"A REAL SOCKEROO!"
Alfred Kazin, *Saturday Review*

"Ms. Dizenzo gives us a girl who is so absolutely alive you walk around feeling responsible for her. *It's just a terrific novel by a terrific writer.*
Harper's

"So heartbreaking, so humorous, and so real. There is the presence of that much-sought, little-found quality called *truth.*"
Chicago Sun-Times

"*Fascinating, sad and funny.* A picture of growing up middle-class in the American fifties that is devastating, both in its authenticity and in its cumulative emotional impact. A writer of major talent. One of the best novels the 1970's has produced so far."
University Review

"*The book flashes with life. . . .* So good it makes you want to run up and down the street thrusting copies into the hands of everybody you ever said hello to and a lot of people you never heard of in all your life. An absolutely remarkable achievement in fiction.
The Cleveland Plain Dealer

Other Avon books by
Patricia Dizenzo

WHY ME? THE STORY OF JENNY   28134 $1.25

an American Girl

by PATRICIA DIZENZO

AVON
PUBLISHERS OF BARD, CAMELOT, DISCUS, EQUINOX AND FLARE BOOKS

FOR C.F.D.

AVON BOOKS
A division of
The Hearst Corporation
959 Eighth Avenue
New York, New York 10019

Copyright © 1971 by Patricia Dizenzo.
Reprinted by arrangement with Holt, Rinehart & Winston.
Library of Congress Catalog Card Number: 76-138871

ISBN: 0-380-00863-7

First Avon Printing, December, 1976

AVON TRADEMARK REG. U.S. PAT. OFF. AND IN
OTHER COUNTRIES, MARCA REGISTRADA,
HECHO EN U.S.A.

Printed in the U.S.A.

Mom was always torturing me talking about all the successful men who proposed to her from the time she was sixteen and the great debutante until she was twenty-two and married Dad. I believed her as she could still easily fool anyone when she wanted to, when sober. People always said what a wonderful mother I had. She said the only man she ever loved was Dad even though he had no money. From hearing them fight I thought they always hated each other. She said I didn't understand love, but someday maybe I would. According to her they loved each other more than ever, in spite of their fights.

When we drove down to Texas to see Granny on Dad's vacation, Mom and Dad sang college songs in the car after drinking a few bottles of beer. They said college years were the best of your life. They talked about their sorority and fraternity, singing the songs of each. They described "hell week." Mom had to hop on one foot and call her sorority sisters "honored madame" whenever she ran into them, plus drop anything she was carrying at their command. They drove Dad out into the country and took all his clothes. He had to get back by getting old clothes from a farmer, hiding behind barns, etc. I always dreaded the idea of college until I found out that some don't allow sororities. Mom described the blackballing system. She told me about the kind of girl who doesn't get asked to join a sorority and it sounded like an exact description of me.

I told her I was going to a college like Celia's that didn't allow sororities. She said I shouldn't worry as she could get me into Theta Omega on any campus. She said, "What's the matter? Afraid of hell week?" I said hell week would be nothing new to me after living with her, I just didn't want to join anything she belonged to. I asked what her major was so I could go into a different field. Unfortunately, it was English, my favorite subject.

I was one of the last girls in my class to wear a bra. I wanted Mom to buy it for me to save me the embarrassment. Mom agreed, suggesting the five and ten in Hackensack. She said she'd buy it but I had to keep her company on the ride back and forth. When we got there she said I should come in the store but I wouldn't have to stay with her. We came to the underwear section and Mom practically shouted out, "Oh, here's one," holding up a bra. I told her just to buy one and not make a scene, and went to the back of the store. I stood around looking at the goldfish, waiting for her to come with the package so we could leave. Suddenly a strange lady tapped me on the back saying, "Is this the young lady?" It was a saleslady, with Mom behind her. I had to walk back to the bra counter with them and pick one out. The lady said I shouldn't be ashamed as it was only nature. Mom smiled, acting like she was well-adjusted like the lady and just wanted to cure me of shyness. I wanted to get three so they would last a while but Mom said no, I should wait and see how this one works out. It wasn't bad looking, though like a lot of Woolworth's stuff it wasn't too sturdy. I got three better ones at Lobell's Youth Center the next day, knowing my right size from the label inside the first.

We all knew Mom drank too much. Even Dad accused her of it all the time, and he didn't even know about the drinking she did in the day. She slept in the afternoon, then took a bath to freshen up before six when he came home. Most of the time Dad didn't suspect anything, but once in a while she did something that made him notice something strange was going on. She liked to drive around, which in her condition was a hazard in New Jersey because of all the highways and high-speed traffic. She usually tried to talk me into going with her, sometimes I went although it was nerve-racking. She drove too fast and I was always afraid she'd be stopped by a cop and arrested for drunk driving. If I argued with her she would just get madder and drive more recklessly. One time when I got home from school she was out and the car was gone. She didn't come home all afternoon. She still wasn't home when Dad got home, and we were getting frantic. About eight o'clock she called from a pay phone. She said she was at a drive-in watching a movie. Dad begged her to come home right away, but she hung up on him. She made a few more calls from different places as she drove around. One time we could hear a lot of trailer trucks over the phone and I was afraid she had pulled over to the side of route 4 or 17. When she finally got home it was about midnight and she was quite drunk. She acted like she'd really had a good laugh on us all. She really was at a drive-in, as I found out the next day. Unfortunately Judy Dorhner (in my class) was there with her sister and saw Mom. She gave me a sly look when she told me, so I guess Mom was making quite a scene.

I always did my homework but I put it off to the

last minute and ended up working till all hours. Once I had to list all the similes and metaphors in *The Odyssey* for an English project, which I put off and had to do the last night. It wasn't so hard, particularly the similes where you just looked for "like" or "as," but it was a lot of writing. Even though I got started at 7:00 (early for me) I was up till about 2:00. After that I still had to iron my gymsuit. I had a gym teacher who demanded spotlessness in sneakers and gymsuit. Every night before gym class I had to iron my gymsuit or I'd get a check the next day. Mom came downstairs while I was ironing. She'd been sleeping a couple of hours and was sober. First she wanted to know what I was doing up so late, then she said I was always doing something boring like ironing. She said when she was my age she attended pajama parties, dances, and sports events. I just kept ironing, feeling like throwing the iron at her. She said I was a wonderful ironer (very sarcastically). I didn't answer her and she just dropped it. She asked me how would I like a milk shake? I agreed and she got some ice cream and Coke, making a soda which she called a brown cow. She had one too. I polished my sneakers with white polish—just washing them didn't make them white enough for Miss Kittrell. Mom said I was the fussiest person she'd ever known. I said it wasn't my idea, if I didn't polish them I'd get a demerit, if I got three demerits I'd fail gym, and if I failed gym I'd be left back and never get out of junior high. She groaned like it was such a bore but she offered to make me a hot chocolate, saying it would help me get a good night's sleep for a change. I agreed even though I just had the soda. She was getting out of her sarcastic mood. She said I should get braces. I said I would if they weren't all over the front, as two of my teeth were coming in crooked. She didn't forget, and the next night she started a fight with Dad about it. He admitted that a couple of my teeth were out of line, but he wanted me to go to a dentist and get them pulled. Mom said it was ridiculous and he should be ashamed to think of pulling two of my permanent teeth. She said if they were gone my front teeth would separate to fill in the spaces, making me gap-toothed. She said I'd look ridiculous and be humiliated when I went to college. She accused him of only thinking about the money. Dad said the expense of an orthodontist was out of the question but Mom won and I got braces practically the next day. It was lucky for me. They were just on the sides so they hardly showed and I didn't mind them at all, and they straightened out my teeth in about one year.

Dad was always hoping Mom would turn into the "ideal wife," just like we hoped she would turn into the ideal mother. He didn't know what to say when she said she was bored to tears. Once he said, what do you think my job is like?

They started drinking when he came home, eating late at night. After drinking a little while they started fighting, sometimes about politics. Mom was a Democrat and Dad was a Republican. Dad furiously shouted that the Democrats were getting us so deep into debt we'd never get out, and then he got on the subject of how she never gave a damn about keeping a family budget and just spent whatever she pleased. He said we were going to end up in the poorhouse. He had to take out a loan from Household Finance, at terrible interest rates. Then he started looking around the room, saying, "Just look at this place!" Whenever he did that I winced, thinking he was looking at the stains on the rug that I never really tried to get out.

There's a good way to get stains out of rugs if you have an un-housebroken dog in the house. Clean it with any kind of rug cleaner, it usually leaves a white spot. Get some dye or tint the same color the rug used to be, apply it to spot with an old toothbrush. Blend in at the edges. Apply tint until the spot is a little darker than the background (it gets lighter when it dries). I used to do this with a blue rug with pink and yellow flowers. It works wonders, at least on rugs with patterns since the match doesn't have to be perfect. I filled in quite a few bad spots once, the rug looked as good as new. I felt great (the spots had been bothering me for months). But then all the dog had to do was carelessly lift his leg against a chair again and I was back where I started, and feeling like a stupid fool for going to so much trouble. And then the rugs had parts worn down to the threads, and they were ugly to start with, so it was a complete waste of time.

Dad accused Mom of giving me too much money for movies. I went Saturdays and sometimes Sunday. She didn't give me any trouble about money (except for clothes). She never kept track of it and always had some dollar bills crammed in her purse. She'd usually fish out a couple for me without any fuss. I liked movies as it was a way to pass the time—I went for escape. I wished my family had the same kind of problems shown in movies. To me it was cheerful that the kids got into trouble and the parents knew best. I never saw a movie about a house like mine—gloominess day in and day out, everything sloppy, always fighting and drinking, and never enough money.

I saw a movie where a girl's life was ruined because she found out her father and mother had adopted her and she wasn't really their own daughter, as she had believed all her life. She found the adoption papers by accident, during a big birthday party being held for her on her sixteenth birthday. If I found adoption papers for myself I'd be glad, as my real parents couldn't be worse than Mom and Dad.

Whenever Mom and Dad had a fight and my name came up, each one talked about me as if I was just like the other. It almost made me laugh, as I'm not like either one of them and I hate them both equally. Dad said I spent too much money, was selfish, and was growing up without learning anything about housekeeping since I didn't have special daily chores. Mom said I was a stuffed shirt, had no personality, was hypocritical, and selfish and arrogant. Each one of them thought I belonged to the other. Dad thought I was a miniature version of Mom, and vice versa. I hated to hear Dad complain about me as I knew he didn't care how much housework I did or how much I had to take from her. He wanted to treat me like a spoiled brat and nothing was going to change his mind. Once I dreamed that Dad's head was as big as the world and I was lost in it. I was running through all the winding alleys in his head, looking for a little doll that looked exactly like me that he kept in a hidden room inside his head and he was twisting out of shape in there. In the dream I had to find the doll, run out of his head with it, and bring it back to life outside. I wished the dream was true and I had a real chance to get away from him. But I didn't know what was in his head and never went near him if I could help it.

I was in the talent show at school, in a dance to "Bolero" with Yvonne Reese and Joan Guerney, choreographed by Mrs. Kern. I was very good friends with Yvonne. "Bolero" started off slow and got faster until at the end it was out of control and we dropped on the floor dead. We rehearsed at lunch period for a few weeks and Mrs. Kern said we were going to be the best thing in the show. I loved dancing as it was a way of expressing my emotions to the world. At the last minute Joan came in with castanets, which she wanted to use in the dance. Yvonne and I said she shouldn't as it would throw everything off. She accused us of just being jealous and threatened to quit. Finally we had to go to Mrs. Kern and tell her. Unfortunately she thought it would be all right if Joan used castanets. But when the show was on, no one could hear them as the music drowned them out.

I had a close call with Mom. When I got home from school she wanted me to get in the car with her and go for a ride. I refused but she persuaded me, saying she wanted to buy me something. I got in and we took off. Mom was in a carefree mood from drinking, and started whizzing along Highland Avenue. She asked me if I needed new loafers, turning my way to look at me as if we were in the back seat with someone else driving. I told her to please keep her eyes on the road. She got annoyed and kept driving the same way. I nervously kept quit, thinking if I said anything she'd explode and get into an accident. She talked about different things she might buy me, saying she saw a factory outlet shoe store on route 4 which she was heading for. As we got to route 4 I was dreading the traffic more than ever. From Highland you had to speed up to get into the whizzing traffic, but Mom thought there was nothing to worry about and just kept chatting while I said nothing. Mom got on 4, making a couple of cars slam their brakes on as she cut over to the left lane. We kept going left, going up the concrete divider with a big bump. It looked like we were going to get stuck on the divider with the tires on both sides, the left ones on the other side of the highway facing oncoming traffic. When Mom cut into 4 I was doing nothing, paralyzed with fear, but finally I snapped out of it, grabbing the wheel from Mom and steering right. We bumped off the divider and got in the left lane again. Some cars were honking their horns but nothing bumped into us. Mom took the wheel again, saying "thank you, darling" as though nothing happened. She wasn't even scared, but she paid a little more attention to the road. A car passed by us and a man swore at us at the top of his lungs. Mom acted like she didn't know why, saying "how rude." Finally we got to "Factory Outlet." Mom made the turnoff okay although she didn't signal. My heart was still beating wildly as I looked at the different counters of shoes. I got a pair of red sneakers. Luckily the store was next to a diner. I asked Mom why not have some coffee before heading home again. I was furious but afraid to show it as we still had the long trip home. Mom had coffee. I had pie and tea. I just talked about anything a mile a minute. She was acting better but I was still afraid if I said anything to criticize her driving it would set her off and make her uncontrollable on

13

the way home. She had two cups of coffee, which sobered her up quite a lot. We stayed about a half hour, until 4:30. I suggested we start home so it wouldn't be too dark. Mom agreed. Going home was much better as she didn't talk too much and watched the traffic, but I was holding my breath all the way. When we got safely home, all my fury at Mom for practically getting us both killed came out, but I was so happy to be home I just forgot it.

We had a special assembly at school and got out early. When I got home a big fight with Mom was in store for me. She was looking in my closet and found a big stack of EC comics I got from Yvonne. Her father knew a dealer so she got them by the dozens. Mom went into an uproar saying they would destroy what was left of my "little mind." She only read one, which she was finishing in a fury when I walked in the door. It had a story by "The Vaultkeeper" about a traveling salesman who stopped at an old farmhouse where an old couple lived. They asked him in, acting like the willing customers, and bolted the door behind him. They told him they liked salesmen but they didn't like to be cheated so they made all salesmen who came by demonstrate their products. They showed him their new electric stove and opened the oven door, showing a dead salesman burnt to a crisp. Then they showed him a washing machine with a dead salesman drowned inside, and a few other appliances, all with dead men inside. They were talking like friendly normal people but naturally the salesman was terrified, knowing he was in the hands of lunatics. They asked him what he was selling and he tried to put them off, saying he left his samples home and had to go. Finally they forced him to open the trunk of his car, where his samples were—electric meatgrinders.

There was another one by "The Old Witch with the Cauldron" about a rich man and his wife who loved to hunt wild animals. They had bear rugs on the floor and elks' heads on the wall for decorations. She had stoles and coats made out of all the different kinds of fur. Hunting was their only great interest in life. Finally they went on a hunting expedition into a jungle where animals were the rulers of men. They wore dead human bodies around their necks as stoles, plus on the floor as rugs and on the walls as plaques. It was the same thing people do with animals without thinking anything of it. Naturally the man and his wife were terrified when they saw, as they knew what the animals were going to do with them for revenge. Mom was in a vicious mood and tore up a few comics right in front of me. I grabbed as many as I could get my hands on—she would have destroyed them all. She accused me of being a little nitwit like all my friends. I begged her not to tear them up, I had to give them back to Yvonne. She said she'd give me to the count of ten to get them out of the house. I ran over to Yvonne's house, which was about six blocks. There was no one at home so I left them in the milk box, feeling relieved to get them safely away from Mom. When I got back she was up in the attic going through a lot of old clothes and junk, looking for books. She found *The Swiss Family Robinson, Robinson Crusoe,* and *Moby Dick* with Dad's name in them. She said those were the books he read when he was my age. I didn't know how he did it even with his intelligence—it was small print and about a thousand pages long each. Maybe it was the only thing he had to do with no television or radio in those days.

Mom said she read *Rebecca of Sunnybrook Farm*, Mark Twain, and different classics when she was my age. She asked me why I deliberately exposed myself to such gruesome filth, trying to make me feel humiliated. She said if that was what I wanted out of life I might as well forget about going to college and meeting nice people. I told her I didn't have time to listen to her lectures as I had Latin homework to do, which she started laughing about very sarcastically. I just tossed off Mom's criticisms and went over to Lois's to do homework. It was introductory Latin and we got easy stories to translate about customs in ancient Rome. They were short easy sentences like in a second-grade reader with "Dick and Jane." If you knew the vocabulary you knew the story in these beginning stories, but the ones at the end looked like murder. As I was walking home from Lois's a car slowed down and it was Dad. He took the car to work. He said to get in, then we drove to Faye's as he had to get cigarettes. While he was in the store, I took a look at Dad's paper. There was a map with the battle line moving back and forth in Korea. The last time I looked we were about in the middle of the country, but this time we were practically in the ocean. I didn't even think about the war most of the time but sometimes I got scared thinking I was living in a fool's paradise. I asked Dad if there was any danger of them coming over here if they pushed us out of Korea. He said no. He said I didn't seem to have any notion of America's industrial might.

The family dentist, Dr. Jack, died so I had to go to a new one, Dr. Emerson. Jack always kept the radio on in his office. He was always singing along and joking, asking me if my boyfriends melted my fillings as he poked around in my mouth, but Emerson was all business. He said I should get two teeth pulled as they had a couple of cavities and the permanent ones were coming in anyway. The nurse called Mom to pick me up as Emerson wanted to give me laughing gas. Mom agreed to come. As I went under with the strange smell of laughing gas I had a dream that Emerson asked me to get in with him in a little pink plane flying to Mars. I agreed. When we got there I stepped out and he quickly flew away into the distance, getting smaller and smaller until he was out of sight. There I was, stranded. When I came out of it, I had two big wads of cotton in my mouth and the nurse was holding my jaw, telling me to bite down. Mom was there. She was trying to act nice but she was drinking. She gave me some comics even though she didn't approve of them, saying I deserved it for what I had been through. Emerson had disappeared. The nurse gave me the two teeth in a Kleenex. Mom said I'd get plenty for them from the Easter bunny. I didn't know if she thought I still believed in that or just said it as a joke. We got into the car, Mom was acting friendly but I was in a daze, not knowing what was going on. Luckily we got home all right (with me paying no attention to Mom's driving) and I jumped into bed and relaxed and read the comics.

Yvonne called me up—she had the idea of going to pick strawberries in a field she knew about. Surprisingly, it was only a couple of blocks from my house. It took us a long time to get across route 17 with all the cars whizzing by. We waited and waited and finally had to get up our nerve and make a dash for it. We were shaking in our boots but it was worth it. There was a big overgrown field by the side of an old rundown house. There were some little strawberry patches spread out all over the ground and some blackberry bushes full of blackberries. Nobody must have come there. I got a little bowl of strawberries and a big one of blackberries which really surprised Mom.

When Dad wasn't yelling at Mom about money or her housekeeping, she was yelling at him about what a failure he was. Dad was a lawyer working in New York in the legal department of Kaiser Steel. Mom said he did more work than anybody but he let people walk all over him and take advantage of him because he didn't have enough backbone to demand more money. According to her he didn't have the nerve to argue cases and just ended up doing a lot of legal research on contracts as other people's flunky. One night she wouldn't get off that subject. She wanted him to demand a raise the next day. He kept trying to hedge, saying yes, but it would take time. She said if he didn't talk to his boss the next day she'd think he was the most spineless coward she'd ever seen. Finally Dad agreed he would.

The next day Mom was nervous and stayed sober, thinking he might call her from the office, but he didn't. When he got home he got a drink as soon as he was inside the door. Mom looked worried when she saw him. When I was upstairs they began to talk about it. Dad had asked for a raise, but didn't get what he wanted. They offered him less money and he accepted it. He told his boss he couldn't support his family on his salary, but his boss, Mr. Furley, said a raise was out of the question. Dad was just about to walk out of Mr. Furley's office when at the last minute he called him back. Dad said, in a relieved way, "If I had closed that door behind me one second faster . . . ," thinking he might have been out of a job, although probably his boss was waiting until the last minute on purpose. Dad seemed to be half happy it was all over, and proud that he got something, and half ashamed he didn't get what he asked for. Mom felt the same way at first, saying it was good he got something, but as the night went on and they kept drinking, she began to change her tune. She said she thought he was going to ask for a thousand more a year, not five hundred. Dad kept saying that was all he could get, and she answered him back very sarcastically and called him a spineless jellyfish. He argued back but in a whining voice. He was never a match for her when she was mad. He could complain but he couldn't really get the upper hand. She kept insulting him and called him a coward and a failure. She said he should get into a private practice or what was the point of being a lawyer. Dad said he didn't have the connections to start a private practice and his best chance was in corporation law. Mom kept calling him a coward. She said she was desperate to get more money and move to a nicer town. After a while Dad stopped saying anything. He went upstairs to his room. We heard him crying in there. Mom came up a little later. She was quite drunk, as we could tell by her steps coming up the stairs. She went into the bedroom and called Dad a big baby. He just kept on crying. Mom was in a really vicious mood. She kept mocking him, calling him a disgusting baby, not a man, and saying he probably wanted his mother. He stopped crying a minute and said, "Please stop, Clare, please stop." She wouldn't, she called him more names. I was afraid he was going to have a heart attack. Dad kept crying, and after a while she stomped out of the room, slamming the door behind her, and went downstairs. I couldn't hear anything from Dad's room and I was afraid he was dead. I opened the door to his room and saw him lying on his stomach on his bed, with all his clothes on and one arm hanging over the edge. He was breathing hard and by the hall light I could see his face was red. I was going to offer to get him some milk, which he had the habit of having with graham crackers before bed. But when he saw me he yelled "Get the hell out of here," probably ashamed to know I heard it all.

He felt like a failure as he didn't make more money. No one in the family was ever supposed to ask how much he made. He worked for Kaiser Steel, probably thinking it would make him as rich as the men who owned their own steel mills in Donora, Pennsylvania where Dad came from. But instead he just made a regular salary. He didn't know why he wasn't more of a success and didn't know what to do about it. He said he could never entertain business associates because of Mom. When I got up the morning after their big fight, he had already left for the office, which was funny considering the state he was in the night before. Sometimes there would be big upsets like that in our family, then everything would go on as usual.

I hated to think of Dad worrying about money and begging for a raise. I wished he had plenty of money and wasn't so dependent on the company and so worried about keeping his job. Mom always said we needed more money, but it wouldn't have made that much difference. The reason we were always in financial trouble was they spent too much on liquor, Mom ran up big telephone bills talking long distance to old friends and arguing with Granny, didn't economize on anything, and things like that. That's why we felt poor and Celia and I didn't have all the right clothes, and the furniture was in terrible shape, with springs sticking out, etc. If we were rich, it would have made a big difference. Then we could have had a housekeeper to keep the house running right, and have meals on time, new house and new furniture, a good psychiatrist for Mom, and my sister, brother and I could have gone away to boarding school. Sometimes I thought about that and made plans about how to get everything set up, but there wasn't any chance we'd ever have that much money, and a little more wouldn't help.

I saw a movie called *M* in a double feature at the Fox, playing along with an Abbott and Costello. It was the story of a man who had the compulsion to murder, played by Peter Lorre. He went into crowds, looking for about fourth or fifth grade girls who weren't with their parents, striking up conversations with them and giving them presents or candy to set their minds at ease.

This movie must have gotten into the "kiddie matinee" by accident. In technicolor it would have been better, even with that plot, but it was in black and white (mostly black) and very slow moving. It was more like a newspaper picture, but moving.

After the murderer struck a few times, the city was in a state of terror. All the families were terrified that their daughters would be next and wouldn't let them go anywhere. The newspapers put pressure on the police to find the murderer, so the police began to search the underworld. This put great pressure on the underworld. Finally the leaders of organized crime met, deciding to find the murderer themselves. They spread a big net through the city and trapped him in a bowling alley. They put him on trial, with criminals for a jury. He pleaded for his life, saying he couldn't help killing any more than other people could help breathing. A spell came over him and he couldn't control himself. He whimpered and cried as he saw there was no escape, begging on his knees. He tried to run away but the mob got out of control and killed him. Sweat was running off his face.

I was home with nothing to do and I read Celia's diary, which she kept in a drawer under her sweaters. I felt guilty but it was so interesting I couldn't stop. She liked a boy in her class and there was a lot in it about him. Everything he said to her she wrote down. They didn't go out on dates (he didn't have a car) but she saw him every day in school and over her girl friend Alice's house where she spent a lot of time. Since she started high school she never came home straight from school. He didn't know she liked him so much. They were "just friends." She was dying to get away to college. She hated Mom but loved Dad. She thought Mom could be a different person if she stopped drinking but she never would. She said Mom was an alcoholic. She said it was driving her crazy to live in the house with Mom and Dad getting worse and worse. There was a lot about how much she loved Dad although he would never know. It was a surprise to me as Celia never told me about her deep emotions. She liked to talk to people her own age (not me). We just talked about what happened in school or different family problems before we went to sleep. We used to fight about what part of the room belonged to who when we were young. I was jealous that she was older. She helped me with my homework when I needed it but I didn't need it too much any more. My main problem was getting down to it. Sometimes she made a lot of jokes about Mom and Dad saying there was a funny side to it all.

Once Mom went into such a deep sleep from drinking that I thought she had died. I got home from school late because I had a late post on safety patrol. It was getting dark and lights were on in most of the houses, but not ours. I knew Mom was home as the car was in the driveway. In the kitchen the shades were down and I couldn't see a thing until I turned on the light. I wondered where Mom was. I thought she was probably asleep on the couch but she wasn't snoring or making a sound. I began to think I shouldn't have come home so late. I found her in the living room, half falling off the couch with her mouth open. I pushed her back up and closed her mouth but she didn't breathe or make a sound or try to brush me away. She was completely limp. I was afraid she was dead. I said to myself, this can't be true.

I shook her by the shoulders, talking like a doctor, praying she'd snap to. Her head kept flopping over. I started crying, asking her to please answer me. I said I'd do anything to bring her back to life. I was remembering all the good things about her, all the times she cooked things for me when she had a hangover and felt terrible. I couldn't believe this was really happening, that I was at school and all the time Mom was dead at home. I shook her again. I tried everything. I yelled to her to get up immediately and then started crying again. After

23

this went on a while, and I had a terrible pain in my throat and was thinking fearfully about what was going to become of the family, Mom came to. She thought I just came in. She started acting like the typical drunk, saying, "What's going on around here. Who turned out the lights?" I was so surprised I could hardly believe my eyes. She got up and started stumbling around, saying, "Oh, hello, darling," in her surprised sophisticated way, as though we just ran into each other at a society ball. In a couple of minutes she was wide awake. I told her it was late and she went upstairs to get dressed. I was furious with her. I started running around straightening up the living room and kitchen, thinking Dad was going to barge in any second. It turned out everything was in pretty good shape, including Mom, by the time he walked in with his usual whistle.

Sometimes I regretted that I ever joined the safety patrol. Peter Ziegler came up with a new rotation of posts that put me back on Oak Street. He was the captain but it was just a popularity contest, he didn't know what he was doing and didn't care. With him as captain we were getting just like the fire partol. I was just finishing the outdoor posts where I was shivering all through the cold spell, and now that I worked my way up to all the inside posts I was back on "the windy corner" on his new rotation plan. I practically froze my feet off on Oak. I had to stand there 8:15 to 9:00 and 3:15 to 3:45, plus noontime, and no one passed by anyway. The only person I could see from Oak was on "railroad," and half the time no one was there, even though they were supposed to signal me off. (Ziegler didn't check posts.) I hated the posts out by Oak and railroad as it was lonely, cold, and nothing to do. I kept looking at my watch and 45 minutes seemed like five hours. I just paced around with my teeth chattering most of the time. I always wanted to come late and leave early but I was afraid the one time I did a first-grader would run across the street, get killed, and it would be my fault and ruin my life. Dad was pretty impressed about my hours "on duty." He said I should wear two pairs of socks inside my boots, which I started doing. A few other kids were steaming too so Ziegler had to change the rotation back. I told him he was crazy if he thought I was going back on Oak Street again. There was no reason for him to change it in the first place so what could he say. He said it was a mistake, he wanted to make the schedules neater to give to Mr. Kaster and he didn't notice he shifted the posts. John Rourke said he should leave that to Bob Downey (assistant captain) and maybe these mistakes wouldn't happen so often.

I had a friend named Beverly, a grade ahead of me. She lived two blocks away, with a conventional mother. Her dresses were always perfectly clean and starched. She was quite carefree, always laughing about nothing. Her mother kept a big jar of cold water in the refrigerator. To me that seemed like unbelievable planning. Besides church and Sunday school, Bev went to Presbyterian Bible class once a week after school. She asked me to come so she could get credit for bringing a guest. I agreed even though I was supposedly an Episcopalian. I didn't care as long as it was Protestant. I was afraid of Catholics but not Protestants as they encourage the independent mind. Episcopalians were the most independent and wouldn't care if you joined or not, but even though all Protestants might not be the same, they wouldn't try to convert you. I had quite a few Catholic friends and was always afraid of being converted. Dad was a Baptist (supposedly) but Celia, me, and the baby were brought up to be Episcopalians even though we didn't go to church that often. When Mom went to church she usually broke out in a sweat in the middle of the sermon and ran out, leaving me there wishing I had the nerve to run out too.

The two ladies who ran the Bible class lived in an old house on a slanty street near some sandpits that weren't built up yet. It wasn't too far from my house but I'd never been out that way. The town had a lot of plans for expansion. They were going to build a housing development there after they filled in the land, so it would be the oldest houses in town next to the newest.

There were about thirty people in the class. I saw one boy from my class (Peter Deller), and also a younger girl a few grades below me. The ladies were sisters. One did all the talking and the other fetched supplies. They had a magnetic board with felt cutouts to stick on it and move around as they told stories from the Bible. Miss Arbut thought the world wasn't real—it was just God's way of testing each person. They sang some Presbyterian hymns, and different members volunteered to read verses, and they took up a collection. Dues were a nickel a week. They had Bible drill, where they called out a book, chapter, and verse in the Old or New Testament. The first one to find it stood up and started reading. The girl who won the first time I was there was an eighth-grader. She was nice looking, kind of thin, blond, and serious. She had nice clothes. I wished I was her, although the next summer she drowned in a lake on the Fourth of July. I wouldn't have known her name, Jennifer Campbell, except that I saw her at that class.

The Bible class had a terrible effect on me. So did the Bible itself, which when I read it for long seemed to tell me to give up all hope. It made me want to run to the movies even though I knew they weren't serious and were only an escape from life. Miss Arbut talked about the crucifixion of Christ, saying we should think about it every day and be grateful as it changed our lives for the better. She showed some pictures and described the crucifixion, which lasted eight hours. I always hated to hear about it in church or anywhere, but no one was upset. It was an old story to them. I began to get the feeling that God was waiting for years to get to me, and that was why he caused Bev to invite me. Now I couldn't get away or pretend I hadn't heard him calling me.

I thought God was telling me I had to go away from the world. He didn't mind seeing me suffer and I shouldn't mind either. I thought I couldn't be happy like everyone else because I had a different view of life, thanks to God. I couldn't see it like anyone else. All the happy things seemed unreal to me, like paper you could just tear up. I thought I had to stop running away to cheerful things, like movies or the Outdoor Girls books, or the radio or friends, and think about the Bible and its lessons. To me the Bible's lesson was you must constantly listen for God's voice and if you give up your whole life to him, doing everything he wants, your reward is you spend the rest of eternity with him. After you die your afterlife goes on forever. You have to give up everything you want if he asks you to, including the idea of ever being happy or having a good time. No one in the class minded that, looking as happy as ever, and I knew I wouldn't either if I didn't know that deep down I hated God and he hated me. Once I asked Mom if it was ever possible to die, after living millions of years in heaven. She said no, I didn't comprehend eternity. I wanted to avoid God and be the typical American girl. I wanted to just eat a lot of junk, be normal, laugh and drive around in a convertible when I was seventeen, go to the movies, and just try to toss off all of Mom's depressions.

But to me the Bible said not to. I thought it proved that nothing in the modern world was reality. It's cheap and flashy and the people who believe in it are in a stupid dream world, even though I envy them. You have to listen to God, think about the Bible, and close your eyes to everything around you, including school and teachers that foolishly say life is easy if you just do what's right. I thought God picked me out because I could take it, but I didn't feel proud. I wanted to be left alone and think about the same things everyone was talking about—like Beverly, who saw every movie and took an hour to tell the story of each, believing they were really true. I believed the Bible was true—depressing, dull, uninteresting, never funny, full of suffering. It was always the story of learning another lesson about how God is the master of all and everyone has to accept it.

I didn't want to eat things like bacon and eggs. I wanted to eat Cheerios because they seemed in another world out of God's control. I thought they were made by people who didn't believe in God. I thought my attitude to life was catching up with me. Mom was drunk all day but I just ran out to play, or I'd just turn on the radio, wanting to hear something exciting instead of her depressing talk. I wanted to keep Mom on the surface and think she wasn't real. I wanted to think school and the radio shows and the typical American family were all that counted. But deep down I knew it wasn't true and I had to stop running away.

It started to rain during Bible class. It got so dark out they had to turn on the lights in the living room although it was only four o'clock. There was flash lightning and thunder. Naturally I thought it was a sign of God's fury. I had an awful feeling I should never have come there but it was too late. Everyone was in the hall, trying to find their coats and getting ready to go, laughing and fooling around, so carefree about life. Some cars drove up outside and the doorbell began to ring. The mother of the boy in my class asked me if I lived on Morgan Street. She said she'd give me a lift home with Peter. I said no, I'd walk. She said that was silly, I'd be soaked to my skin. I thought God was telling me I had to run out into the storm and leave the warm house, the lights, the people, even though I would have given anything to stay. I knew I couldn't go with her though it seemed so easy. I was more afraid of everyone noticing me than I was about going out under the trees. I just said I'd be all right and left the house right away, trying to beat everyone out. It was raining cats and dogs. I ran across the street into the empty lot, hoping no one would see me. It was even worse than I thought it would be. The grass was soaked and slippery so I had trouble running. Every step or two I landed in a little puddle and completely soaked my shoes. I wanted to get out of sight of everyone so they wouldn't think I was crazy. I thought God was waiting for me in the middle of the sandpit and might even appear to me, although I dreaded the idea. Thunder kept cracking from the sky as though lightning was splitting the trees.

I started down a slope leading from the lot to the sandpit. It wasn't really sand, but quite overgrown. Later they made a little league park out of that part. There was high wet grass higher than my knees, big weeds, some bushes, and some tiger lilies. There were no real paths. The part I was in led to another built-up old street about four blocks from my house. Even though I was only about a block away from houses and lights, I thought I was at the end of the world. Every time it thundered I thought lightning was going to strike me. I tried to pray, saying, "God, what do you want of me?" I would have said I wanted to go home, but I was afraid to. I was soaked to the skin and running around although I didn't know where I was going, and getting scared because it was getting darker by the minute. I was terrified about getting electrocuted by lightning. Then I saw a hill ahead of me and a little foot trail going up it. It looked like a yellow line in the grass. The grass was all grey, not green, swinging around in the wind. The path was just about twenty feet away. There was a wood fence running along the top. I felt relieved, as if God was giving me a sign I could go home. I could hardly believe my eyes, the grass was turning black, I expected the path to disappear but it didn't. I ran up it and climbed over the fence, it wasn't high. I was at the end of a dead-end street not too far from my house. I recognized it because I was once there selling magazine subscriptions for the fire patrol.

As soon as I was out of the sandpit I wasn't worried. The sight of the houses and the lights in the windows calmed my nerves. I ran along the street wanting to put the sandpit behind me. I thought I could have died there. I began to worry again when I got near my house, running all the way. I was afraid it wasn't really over. There was a little light coming from our living-room window, showing how dirty the venetian blinds were, and Mom was standing at the door for some reason. She looked beautiful to me. Then I thought God was screaming at me to get down on my knees on the sidewalk in front of our house and walk to the house like that. I thought I'd better, although I was afraid Peter's mother might be driving past any minute on their way home. I knelt down fast and started walking to the house on my knees, trying not to scrape them, then thinking I shouldn't care. I was already so soaked it didn't matter how much of a mess I was. Mom didn't know it was me at first, but then she recognized me. She said, "What in heaven's name are you doing?" I just kept trying to reach the steps, laughing as though it was just a trick I wanted to try. Mom said, "What on earth are you doing?" I felt ashamed but I just laughed as though it was a trick. She said she'd never seen it pour like this. She said, "Darling, you're soaked to the skin." She said I'd better get my wet things off right away. She had just taken a nap and was sober. The thunder woke her up. She looked and acted quite nice, but also worried and afraid of something as she always was when she wasn't drunk. She didn't know where I was, although I told her about the Bible class that morning when I asked her for money for dues. She said she'd better straighten up the house before Daddy came home. She asked me if I'd do the living room and the beds while she did the kitchen. She said she'd make some hot tea for the two of us to have together. I was sorry Dad had to come home and she'd be drinking whiskey again in a couple of hours.

I had a dream about Mom. She was lying on the couch in the living room, and all of a sudden she got up and walked out the front door. She walked to the end of Morgan Street, crossed route 17, and kept walking. I followed her. She walked past houses I'd never seen before, then no houses. We were out in the country walking on a dirt road. All we saw were old broken-down farms once in a while. There were no people or cars around. I wanted us to head back but she didn't hear anything I said. She was in a trance. I tried to grab her hand but it slipped through me like a ghost, so I couldn't get a grip on her or make her listen. I was worried we'd never get back home. It kept getting more empty and completely quiet. I thought there weren't any places like this left but it seemed to go on forever. Then all the color went out of everything. I could only see Mom and me and everything in black and white.

I was trying to persuade her to go back home. She just kept gliding along the ground, looking straight ahead as if she saw someone there. I had to run to keep up but I wanted to go back and kept looking over my shoulder. I was afraid she might disappear into thin air any minute and I'd be lost out there. Then Mom jumped into the air and landed in a field, turning into a scarecrow. I turned into a crow and flew away.

Someone else in my class had an alcoholic mother—Karl Rovere! I found out from Celia—Karl's older sister was in her English class. They had to write character sketches. Celia said Marion Rovere wrote one about a fat lazy slob who sat around the house all day. The only thing she would get up for was to get more pretzels and beer. She wrote like a scientist describing a strange specimen. No one knew it was her mother but Celia heard from some kids in their neighborhood that Mrs. Rovere was fat and never went out of the house. Karl was the genius of the class. He came into the class in fifth grade, during science. We had to give oral reports on current events in science for Miss DePauw. Karl volunteered to give a report with no preparation. It was on archaeology, about a recent expedition where they found the remains of a primitive tribe in New Guinea. He was really interested in it, using his hands to make illustrations of bones, etc. An adult in this tribe was only about the size of a fourth-grader. The report was far better than the ones we were used to, and he became known as the class "brain." In the sixth grade the class had a talent show and Karl turned out to be a terrific tap dancer. Most of the time he didn't care about making friends or having a good time. At spelling bees he spelled the first word wrong on purpose and sat down and slipped out a book. I saw a picture of him when he was young. We all had to write our autobiographies for Miss Garvey and use pictures to show the different stages of our lives. I looked at his with Judy Dorhner. In the picture he was playing in the snow with his sister, Marion Rovere. They both looked happy and healthy, with rosy cheeks. Judy said he was cute in the picture but you'd never recognize him now.

He was terrific in math, his favorite subject. It was my worst subject. It gave me a headache and made me feel like a fool for trying. I didn't like to strain my mind with math or even think about it. To me the numbers were like ghosts. At school they seemed to silently say everything is easy, like two and two is four, but mock you when you were alone, saying "a lot of good it'll do you." They were like the sphinx or like a living room would be with no chairs or couches but only a number 4 or 5 in the corners, and only a 7 or 8 lying on its side for the housewife.

I told Celia I read her diary. It was late as she was up a long time doing her homework. She probably thought I was asleep. When she put everything away and stacked up her books I told her. She was mad and started shaking me by the shoulders, saying why couldn't I ever keep my nose out of things. She said I had to promise never to tell Dad about it (I wouldn't anyway). After a while she calmed down. She said at least I admitted it but I had to promise never to go into her things again, as she needed a little privacy. I was really relieved. I told her I had some of the same emotions about the family.

Bob Cerano had a birthday party after school and I was one of the few girls invited. He was a new boy who lived in the new development. His house was where the old sandpits used to be. I remembered my run into the woods after Bible class and wondered if any of the people there knew they were living on "holy ground." Bob's mother was young, with red hair. She had a little boy, about two, who also had red curly hair. Bob must have taken after his father. Mrs. Cerano sat in the dinette feeding the baby while the party went on in the living room. We played the usual party games and had ice cream and cake. I was pretty popular. It was a fairly small party, about fifteen people, mostly in my class but some younger ones from Bob's neighborhood.

About 5:30 everything began to break up. I called Mom to pick me up, thinking she'd be awake. I didn't want to walk home from the development where I really didn't know my way around. It was cold out. She sounded all right on the phone and agreed to come. When the car pulled up and I got a look at her, I could tell she was drinking. To my horror a lot of kids asked for a ride home. She said sure and I couldn't think of any way to stop it. Seven kids and me piled into the car. Mom thought she was fooling everyone by her cheery manner. The kids didn't pay too much attention to her at first. We ran into trouble because of how the development was laid out—not in blocks but winding circles that lead to dead-ends half the time. To make things worse the houses were alike except for little differences in the shutters or window boxes, etc. Mom drove around and soon the boys started yelling and laughing that we'd already passed the houses we were passing. I prayed we'd get out without too much trouble. Mom kept driving around in circles. We drove into some dead ends which were murder to turn around in, and once again passed by some houses we'd seen before, including the Cerano's house. I saw Mrs. Cerano again through their big living-room window. Mom wasn't embarrassed because she thought she was acting perfectly sober but everyone else began to think it was getting ridiculous. We came to a fork in the road and the boys in the car yelled "turn" and she went left, then they all laughed and yelled "no, no, the other way." She tried to turn right but couldn't make it. Then she had to back up, blocking two cars which started honking, while she maneuvered around, swearing under her breath all the time. When she was finally headed straight, the street turned out to be a dead end. She went up a driveway to back away but she was way off and left tire tracks on the lawn. We got two big jolts as she went up and down the curb. I was afraid the people were going to come running out of the house, but no one did. We got away fast. Everyone was doubled over with laughter. I couldn't tell if they knew she was drunk or just thought it was funny. I felt so mortified I wanted to get out of the car but I looked out the window, acting like nothing was happening. We got lost again, passing the Ceranos' house again and also the house with the tracks on the lawn. Finally we got out of the development and on the regular roads. We let the seven kids off at their houses, one by one. No one wanted to be first so there was a lot of arguing and confusion. Each time someone got out I breathed a sigh of relief. It seemed like a year to me until we got to the last boy's house.

We were the last people on our block to get television. Mom and Dad said they only ran programs for idiots but after a couple of years they broke down and bought one anyway. TV cut down on the fights although Mom got bored and restless after an hour or so, saying she couldn't stand it. She said we were getting to where we never said a word to each other (probably just as well). She thought Milton Berle was an idiot. Dad drank a lot and watched it till about 10:00 or 10:30, then he went to bed. He said he needed to relax and get a good night's sleep for the next day. Unfortunately I couldn't watch TV with Dad in the same room. It got on my nerves for some reason and I couldn't concentrate. Usually I watched the late movies if there was no school the next day, with Celia or by myself after she went off to college. The baby watched the kid shows in the afternoon plus old westerns, so there was always the noise of gunfire going through the house then.

I was best friends with a girl in my class named Lois Barres. She lived just a block away, which was lucky. Her mother died when she was a baby, her father moved to Cleveland, and she lived with her grandparents. She wore a bra about a year before I got mine. She had a nice room of her own with a phonograph and all the latest records. I went over there and we played Joni James and Johnnie Ray, who were all the rage. She sent off for a picture of Johnnie Ray and surprisingly got a big one in the mail signed "All my love, Johnnie" (probably signed by someone else). Lois was the kind who was dying for love. She liked one boy after the other, talking about him all the time and crying if she saw him with another girl. Some girls in my class (Maureen Daly and her crowd) said she was going to get in a lot of trouble if she wasn't in it already. I felt sorry for her as she was an only child and her grandparents were too old to notice her, plus hard of hearing. I hated to hear her talking like it was the end of the world whenever her boyfriend talked to another girl. Sometimes I was afraid I'd get so desperate for love I'd fall in the gutter and never get up.

She failed algebra and I tried to give her homework help even though I hated math. It was partly to pay her back for letting me come over and partly an excuse to come over more. Her grandparents never cared and couldn't hear any noise from her room, so a few times when things were too loud at home I wangled an invitation from her. I went over a lot after Celia went to college as I was lonely without her jokes. Lois didn't understand the basic steps of algebra. I explained an easy example again and again, saying if x plus 2 equals 3, then subtract 2 from each side and x has to equal 1. She said she understood but then she couldn't do a problem just like it, x plus 4 equals 5. She just guessed at the numbers. I said imagine a seesaw with a box on each end, containing five balls each, all the same size. It balances because the boxes weight the same. Now if you take a ball off each side, it will still balance, won't it? Or if you add two balls to each side? As long as it's the same. She said yes but she didn't really understand it. I knocked myself out trying to show her, knowing even a baby could see it, but then I realized she just didn't care.

Once Mom took me to a circus (just me). Two clowns were standing by the entrance—the two opposites. One was fat and jolly, wearing a white clown suit with big red polka dots. He had a sparkling magic wand which he ran around with trying to touch people. The other clown was miserable, dressed in a tramp's outfit with soot all over his face, and a big white frown painted on.

I dreaded holidays because the family had to go through the traditions. We always had a turkey on Thanksgiving, etc. One Thanksgiving (when Celia came home on the first vacation from college) Mom and Dad got drunk quite early in the day. The idea of all five of us having dinner together was getting more and more like a joke, but Mom already had the turkey in the oven. Finally around six o'clock we all had to sit at the table, acting like the typical family on Thanksgiving. Mom asked me to say grace, which she knew I hated to do. Dad sat there with a stupid smile on his face. Mom staggered in with a turkey sliding all over one of her tarnished silver family heirlooms. Dad carved it. As soon as he sliced it we could see the turkey was practically raw underneath, but Mom and Dad acted like nothing was wrong. She must have put the oven on too low or forgotten to defrost the turkey. I felt disgusted. When Celia got her plate she just looked at the meat, saying, "Now isn't this lovely? Isn't this a wonderful Thanksgiving? And what a turkey!" The whole thing struck her funny. She started laughing and laughing. I did too. Celia got up from the table saying it was ridiculous and we should forget the family dinner. Dad got disgusted, saying, "Oh, what's the use?" He stalked out into the sun parlor and watched the football games on TV. Mom acted like she didn't know what was wrong with everyone. I suggested that she go upstairs and take a nap, and she agreed. Celia was still laughing. She said we should get everything cleared up. I helped her get the dining room and kitchen straightened up, which took a couple of hours since everything was a mess and I even washed the floor. Celia cleared off a place near the sink for John and gave him silverware to dry as she washed it. I cleaned the stove and refrigerator and straightened out the shelves and took out the garbage. She cleaned all the pots and pans and so on. When everything was done, she sliced some of the raw turkey and fried it in a pan with melted butter. She didn't know how to cook but it turned out quite well. We had that with cranberry sauce and canned sweet potatoes. We had a terrific time laughing about the whole day, which started out so depressing. Everything was cheerful and we had a terrific dinner, thanks to her idea for cooking the turkey.

For dessert we had pumpkin pie which Mom had got at the bakery. Celia and I had coffee and she made John hot chocolate. She asked him if he wanted an apple. She told him a joke about a person who wanted to eat a dozen apples because he thought if an apple a day keeps the doctor away, then a dozen would keep a dozen doctors away. John laughed at that about five minutes. He started coughing and she had to pat him on the back. He kept laughing, looking like he was going to roll off the cupboard. It wasn't too funny but I guess it was the first joke he ever got. Dad came in to see what was going on and we made a plate for him. He put a damper on everything but finally he said he was going to take a nap.

After Dad went to sleep Celia got the idea of us going to the movies (her and me). Then hating the idea of suddenly leaving John flat when he was having such a good time, she said why not take him along too. I only had a dollar but Celia laughingly said she would go on a "raid" and get more. She came downstairs waving a five-dollar bill. We put a sweater on the baby, Celia wore her "alma ma-ter's" sweatshirt, and I wore her old Hackensack High sweater. We took the 44 to Main Street and ran to the Fox, with Johnny holding hands in the middle. When we got there the first show was over but we were in time for the second, *The Invasion of the Body Snatchers*. There weren't any "Thanksgiving crowds" at the theatre. It was pretty empty. We sat near the back with no one close by so we could talk and fool around. We were all hungry again, surprisingly, so we got popcorn. We had a great time. Celia seemed happy to see us again. Johnny kept laughing and smiling and eating his popcorn and asking for more. I got him another box.

The movie was about invaders from another planet who took over the bodies of earth people. They had big pods about the size of watermelons which they planted in people's homes. The pods began to grow into an exact duplicate of someone in the house. Then when the person was sleeping the pod could take over his body, the person was dead and it was just an alien walking around in his body. It started out with "mass hysteria," dozens of people were saying something was different about someone in their family. They didn't know what, but it was as though it wasn't really the same person. Naturally it sounded ridiculous. Only one person suspected what was going on (a doctor). One of his patients was very upset, saying her husband was suddenly like a stranger. It wasn't really her husband even though he looked just the same. It was like something evil in the house and she thought she was going crazy. The next day she said smiling, "Oh, he's fine. Forget all the silly things I said," walking calmly by him on the street. She told the doctor not to worry so much. He began to think it wasn't really his patient but a pod person. An old man told the doctor that his wife didn't seem like herself any more. He knew something was wrong but couldn't put his finger on it as she looked the same. This confirmed the doctor's suspicions that she had become a pod person, but the next day he went to see the man and he said his wife had just been a little sick but now she was her old self again. He told the doctor to calm down and not worry so much. He was a pod person now, trying to put the doctor off the track. This happened to the doctor's best friend and his wife, the town psychiatrist, and the police. The pod people wanted to make everyone like them. They didn't have deep feelings and thought it was better that way. The doctor and his fiancée hated the idea and were determined to save the world from them, but no one believed their story. Finally the whole town had become pod people and they were tracking them down (the doctor and his fiancée) as they were the only humans left. His fiancée said, "I don't want to be like them, like vegetables. I want to have deep feelings. I want to love and be loved!" Celia laughed and waved her arms around her head, saying, "Me too! I want to love and be loved!"—just kidding around in the empty theatre. They couldn't fall asleep because that's the only way their bodies could be taken over. They escaped from the town with the mob on their trail and hid out in a cave. They were both getting sleepy but they were afraid to fall asleep. The doctor had to leave her to find help, warning her not to fall asleep. He heard beautiful music but it turned out to be a car radio. When he came back she started saying, very tenderly as if she really loved him, that they ought to think about the problem some more, maybe they were being too hasty and the pod people weren't so bad. To his horror he realized that she had fallen asleep and a pod person was in her body trying to win him over. She looked just the same, but there was something different and he almost went crazy thinking he couldn't trust anyone. It ended with him trying to warn the world, but everyone thought he was crazy. Then he discovered some trucks crossing the state line loaded with pods, which everyone laughed about saying they were just watermelons, until they opened one and found out they weren't.

I used to be afraid of Mom and she forced me into a lot of things I didn't want to do. I didn't know about her drinking or even know what drinking was then. When Celia was in school and I didn't go yet, Mom had no one around but me and she got a lot of harebrained schemes. One was for me to make a plaque of my handprint to give Dad. She got in the car and bought plaster of Paris, which we mixed up in the basement. She said this was a wonderful experience for me, probably talking to herself. She made a big ball of plaster of Paris for me to make my handprint on. She described how plaster of Paris is used for casts and dries quickly. At the last minute I got scared and refused to put my hand in it. Mom lost her temper. She swore a blue streak at me, grabbing my hand and pushing it down on the plaster. Then I had to paint it blue and give it to Dad, who asked what it was for. She wanted me to learn ballet too, so she got me in the car and drove to a ballet school. She told the lady that I was her little girl and she wanted to enroll me in the school. The lady said there were no classes that day as they were having a recital with all classes participating. Mom wanted me to be in the recital but the lady said no, I could start with a new class the next week. Mom wouldn't take no for an answer. She insisted I should be in the recital, saying it would be a wonderful experience for me, even though I never had lessons. The lady said they didn't have a costume for me at this short notice. Mom insisted and the lady said she'd look. All the time I was whispering to Mom that I wanted to go home and she was ignoring me. I was afraid to argue for fear she'd lose all her self-control and make a scene in front of everyone. They hemmed a skirt for me just in time. The recital was in a big room with ballet practice bars around the walls and a lot of mothers and visitors sitting on one side of the room. There was a girl playing the piano in the corner. The different classes were lined up against the bars, oldest to youngest. I was with the beginners. We all had red short skirts and white cotton tops. The ballet teacher walked down the line putting each girl's leg up on the bar. My leg wouldn't stretch up so high and he tried to force it. I tried to go along but it hurt too much and I couldn't stand it. I started crying and ran crying across the room to Mom, who was sitting with the other mothers. She was full of sympathy, hugging and kissing me, saying "There, there, Mama understands." She said the man was terrible to force my leg. She made quite a scene showing how understanding she was. She didn't mind people looking but I was ready to go through the floor. I kept looking at my leg until we were out of the room. Why did she think it would be a wonderful experience? Did she think I could pick up ballet from looking at the others ahead of me in line, or did she think it would be good to show someone who didn't know ballet next to ones who did? We left the place and I begged her never to make me go back again. She agreed.

Another time she took me to an amusement park. There was a popcorn man there and Mom bought a box. We sat on a bench to eat it and Mom discovered the melted butter was only on the top. She told me to ask the man for more. I knew he wouldn't agree and I didn't want to ask. I never had her nerve. She said I was afraid of my own shadow and pushed me around a little, so I went over to the man. When I asked for more butter he started swearing at me, saying I had a hell of a nerve and telling me to get the hell out of there. When I told Mom she said she never heard of such a rude person. We went on "The Bug." It wasn't too bad, but a little on the fast side. I was at the age where I liked the merry-go-round, which Mom said was for sissies. "The Bug" lurched around and you had to hold onto something, and all I had was Mom, who I was afraid might stand up to show off. She said not to tell Dad because he'd be furious and think it was too dangerous, which made me worry and cry as I thought I always had to tell him the truth. Mom never worried about danger. Once she rented a bicycle and made me ride on the back. I didn't want to but she called me a sissy, so I reluctantly agreed. We went down a hill on the bike and my ankle got caught in the spokes. There was blood all over the place and it hurt like hell. Mom dramatically carried me up the hill to the house. Her brother my uncle Tyler was visiting and he even yelled at her for putting me on a bicycle when I was too young. If only he'd been around before. I had to get six stitches. Mom acted sorry but like it was just one of those things, not her fault. All those times she was drinking and looking for trouble but I didn't know it. Another time she wore golf shoes with cleats in the house. She walked all over the place making marks on the rug and laughing.

Mom and Dad discussed politics and the subject of McCarthy came up. Mom said everyone was getting afraid to criticize the government for fear he'd call them a Communist and splash their names all over the headlines. She said he was a danger to the country but at least there was something interesting on TV for a change. Dad said he wasn't really serious about Communism and just pulled a lot of harebrained stunts to get attention, as a

Senator he was a joke. He didn't know how to conduct himself in Congress and could never keep a job in business. After a while they got on the subject of Mom's relatives. Dad criticized her father, saying he wasn't cut out to be a farmer (he used to be a professor). Something often went wrong with his crops. He once wrote Mom asking for $100 and Mom wrote out a check without telling Dad but he found out soon enough as it bounced and the bank called him at work. Dad said Mom had to consult him about those things. It ended in a fight but it was over early as Mom went upstairs to bed around nine, right before "Our Miss Brooks." Dad stayed in his chair watching it. He was in a bad mood, not saying anything. I finished my homework early and set my hair, not expecting anything to happen—then Dot Schaeffer unexpectedly called. We had to do a dramatic reading of "The Congo" the next day for English. We were supposed to meet before school to practice but she was getting nervous and wanted to decide how to divide the lines and practice on the phone. She was afraid if we didn't get it right it would sound ridiculous. I couldn't get her off the phone although Dad was steaming in the living room. The phone was in the dining room with no door to shut. She didn't want to say any of the refrains by herself. We split up the lines (me agreeing with everything Dot said) and read about four pages but I could hardly hear myself think. Dad was giving me menacing looks as I read the refrains, "Boom-lay, boom-lay, boom-lay, boom," and I was afraid he was going to get up and murder me when the commercial came on, not caring what you could hear on the phone. Dot kept wanting to go back over parts, talking about whether we should have a long pause after the first verse or a short one, etc. Finally, really getting scared, I told her my father had to make an emergency call. She wanted to come over but couldn't get a ride from her older brother, thank heavens. When I got off the phone I ran upstairs and Dad didn't say anything.

I had to meet Dot at 8:00 by her locker which meant catching the early bus. I hated that bus as it meant leaving the same time as Dad and bumping into him, but I got to sleep early so I wasn't too tired. Dot was a nervous wreck in the morning and she got me all upset before English. Naturally Bob Cerano and Norman Brentzel were laughing in the back trying to make us feel ridiculous. Bob could always make me laugh when I was trying to be serious but not this time so the reading was fine. Miss Garvey said it sounded like we practiced a lot. We gave the reading first so we could relax the rest of the period. Joan Guerney gave a book report on the autobiography of Helen Keller. You'd think someone in her shoes would have given up, with no sight and no hearing it was amazing she learned so much. Miss Garvey said her example should make us ashamed of ourselves as we didn't have her handicaps but we still didn't get that much accomplished. Bob Cerano raised his hand and said the trouble was we didn't have that great devotion from our teachers, everybody raised their hands to agree and soon the whole class was laughing, including Miss Garvey.

I was runner-up in the school spelling bee. Yvonne won it. We both had to go to the Bergen County Annual Spelling Competition, which was held at night in Clifton. Our mothers had to go with us and Miss Geller, the principal. Mom was sober and looked quite nice. I wore my blue skirt with new white blouse. I sat in the audience with Mom and Miss Geller, and Yvonne sat on the stage with the winners from other schools. I was supposed to be the substitute if Yvonne got sick. She dropped out on the third round. I was glad I didn't win the school competition in Somerset as I would have missed the first word she got, "oxymoron." The words they asked were ridiculous. I hadn't even heard of half of them. The people who survived to the last rounds must have studied spelling from the dictionary, not just picked it up from reading, school, etc. I thought I could bone up in about a year if Mom would quiz me on three trick words a night, going through the dictionary that way. Celia said don't kill yourself to be an expert in spelling, it isn't worth it. One night Mom taught me a few long words, like "antidisestablishmentarianism." I kept asking her for long words but she couldn't think of many others. She gave me "infantile paralysis" but then said it was two words. I didn't have any regrets—the winner of the Bergen County match had to go to a state competition, and the winner of that went on to the U.S. championship competition. I would have hated sitting on all those stages, shaking in my shoes, getting words I'd never heard of and trying to guess how to spell them. Mom was acting nice. She whispered in my ear there were a lot of things better than being a "quiz kid." Yvonne's mother was disappointed when Yvonne dropped out, but Mom told Yvonne she did fine and shouldn't give it another thought. I felt proud of Mom, wishing she was always like that. She was sober and just like any other mother, but with more personality. Miss Geller was grumpy that our school didn't win the county championship but she agreed with Mom that it wasn't everything. Mom said we should all go out for ice cream and it was her treat. We stopped at Holly's on Route 4 and had sundaes. Mom was like a different person and I kept looking at her, trying to figure her out. When Miss Geller dropped us off at our house, Mom practically ran into the living room with a big sigh of relief. Dad laughed, saying, "I'll bet I know what you could use," meaning a drink. Mom said she was about to die and gulped one down in the kitchen. They were laughing and hugging each other. They thought it was a terrible experience to attend an event like that. Mom said it would take a week to get over it. For once Dad sympathized with her. They went up to bed. I was excused from homework but I wasn't sleepy so I decided to read the story we had for English, "The Masque of the Red Death." I started to make some hot chocolate but Mom's big bottle of sherry was staring me in the face when I looked for the cocoa. I poured a glass to see what it was like. Mom drank sherry or chablis in the day and whiskey at night with Dad. She got gallon jugs of Gallo wine, saying it was the cheapest form of alcohol you could find anywhere. I didn't like sherry but I wanted to see what it did to me. I drank a glass a little at a time, wondering if it would give me a warm feeling and make all my worries go away. I thought Mom and Dad would kill me if they saw me, or go crazy worrying that I had turned into an alcoholic at my age. I finished the glass off in a couple of big swallows and started staggering around the living room, but I was just fooling around, not really drunk.

It was my birthday, which I thought Mom forgot but she surprised me by getting cake and ice cream for the family. We had it when Dad came home. It was two Nancy Drews from Mom, *Champion's Choice* from Dad, Friendship's Garden cologne from Celia, plus some checks in the mail from different relatives.

We were getting first-aid lessons from Miss Cross, the school nurse. She taught us the basic steps of first aid—how to give artificial respiration, how to treat shock by keeping the victim wrapped in a blanket, not to move a person who was in a car accident as he might have internal injuries, and a few others. We hated first aid as Miss Cross was very strict in class. She resented the nickname of Mary Marvel, sending Bob Cerano to the principal's office for saying it as a joke as she walked in the first class with her long blue cloak over her nurse's uniform. (She almost got him suspended.) We were expecting a class like Miss DePauw's, with a few jokes allowed, but Miss Cross was all business. Miss DePauw was the most popular teacher in the school. She loved science and tried to make it as interesting as possible, telling about current events in science and new inventions. She said Louis Pasteur did much more for humanity than Napoleon. We kidded around quite a lot in her class. She resented Miss Cross because we had first aid once a week during science period. The last week of first aid we learned how to treat snakebite by applying a tourniquet, cutting an X over the fang marks and sucking out the poison. Miss Cross said none of us knew how to tie a tourniquet right and no one understood the pressure points so she was requesting a four-week extension of the first-aid course because of our poor progress. We told Miss DePauw in science and she exploded as it meant Miss Cross taking over more of her science periods. She sarcastically said she was glad Miss Cross was teaching us how to treat snakebite as there were probably about three rattlesnakes in Bergen County. It was a teacher's feud. Everyone laughed at Miss DePauw's jokes, it was a relief from Miss Cross. She put us through surprise practical exams—suddenly you had to tie a tourniquet on someone as she held a stopwatch.

Miss DePauw said she was going to the principal's office to get the matter settled, she said the snakes in New Jersey were so old and confused by the traffic all you had to do was slap them. She was steaming about Miss Cross but she liked to joke in our class as she knew we were on her side. She went to Miss Geller's and demanded that the first-aid course be over as it was cutting into her teaching plan for science. Miss Cross just got one more week. At the last class she said if we were ever in any accidents she hoped we remembered more than we showed in our practical exams. Too bad we didn't get the certificates she promised, but at least first aid was over.

I wanted to redecorate the house to be ready in case I ever had to ask anyone over. I thought there would be nothing to hanging wallpaper and begged Mom to let me start with her room, which I had always wanted to redecorate. I thought if I could change a few things around her, everything would be all right. When I learned knitting for the Red Cross at school I made her a blue sleeveless sweater, thinking if she wore it with a white blouse she'd stop drinking and always look presentable. Mom reluctantly agreed and bought the paste, brushes, and wallpaper. I picked out the design, long-stemmed rosebuds on a light blue "quilted" background. I took off a day from school so I could have a whole day without Dad around to interfere. The first strip was the hardest, as I didn't know how to measure it, slide out wrinkles, and get out the air bubbles. I practically went crazy, having to run up the ladder to fix it at the top, then run down again to fix it at the bottom, etc. When I finally got it straight Mom was really impressed, saying it looked like a professional job. She said we really ought to hand it to ourselves. She was helping, but leaving most of it for me. Then I realized that the design was upside down. The roses were falling down with the stems up, and it looked ridiculous. Mom said what was the difference? She said we'd be crazy to take it down after all our trouble. I pulled it off before the paste could get dry, telling Mom that we still had to cover four walls and we shouldn't do it all wrong just to match one strip. I told her it would drive anyone crazy to be in the room with the design like that. She had to agree since I took it down before she could talk me out of it, saying she didn't know what made me such a perfectionist but she had to admire me for it. Once I got the hang of it, it began to go quicker. I fitted the pieces around the doors and windows by folding the paper against the woodwork and cutting it with a razor blade along the fold line. Mom kept me company and helped mix the paste, and smoothed down the paper on the bottom while I was on the ladder doing the top. She kept saying who could have believed we could do such a professional job. I felt great as it was a neat job and the paper covered up a lot of chinks in the walls which I filled in with spackle. Mom kept going in and out, in quite a good mood. She was drinking and wasn't much help toward the end, but she kept praising me and saying Dad wouldn't believe his

52

eyes. She brought me a Coke and a peanut butter sandwich and went off in the living room to take a nap. I turned on the radio. When it was 3:10, and I was just thinking of school letting out, I was on the third wall, which only had one window and was smooth sailing. The room was beginning to look terrific, bright and flowery instead of the dirty light green it used to be. I took a break now and then, drinking Coke and listening to the radio. I felt like I was hanging roses around Mom and Dad on all sides and it was going to change their life. It was getting dark when I got to the fourth wall, which was small but had two doors. Dad came home just before I finished the whole job and was tremendously surprised. He said he thought wallpaper was impossible except for a professional but he had to admit there weren't any mistakes. I felt great and even thought of doing odd jobs for other people to make extra money. By the time I cleaned the floor and moved all the furniture back, it was about 8:00. I took a bath and called up Joan to get the homework. I had all my books home. Fortunately there wasn't too much and I finished it by 11:00. When I went to bed I felt tired and quite sore from all the stretching. I had a backache and got the hot water bottle to sleep with.

I had one beautiful outfit for school—a red and blue plaid wool pleated skirt, worn with a matching belt and red sweater, but everything else in my wardrobe stank. I had a black straight skirt, a navy blue, two white blouses (not that white), a green sweater, and that was it. They were all basic clothes so I could switch around. I had three cinch belts, one black, one red, and a striped one Mom picked up for me that didn't go with anything. I felt desperate because everything I had was so ugly but Mom said the family was in debt and couldn't afford more clothes for me. I got a few of Celia's old things. I wanted to wear the red and blue outfit every day but I was afraid of getting tired of it. Nothing fit me right as my skirts were too loose at the waist, causing my blouses to come out unless I wore a cinch belt, which gave everything a bunched-up look at the waist. My skirts were gabardine and got wrinkled as soon as I sat down, which made them and me look horrible. I would have been better off in jumpers—too bad I didn't have any. Mom bought me a ridiculous peasant blouse with green and yellow embroidery all over it and big puffy sleeves. She said it caught her eye and she thought it would look nice on me. Naturally I couldn't wear it to school. I was furious because it cost five dollars and I saw a beautiful plaid skirt in the Rainbow Shop in Hackensack for exactly five dollars but I couldn't buy it. For three more I could have gotten a matching yellow sweater, or worn it with my green sweater. Mom acted hurt that I didn't like the blouse. How ridiculous it looked with a drawstring neck and those sleeves. I begged her to give me the money if she ever had any extra for my clothes, but she didn't like the idea.

No one at school thought I was clothes conscious. I wouldn't be if I stayed home every day like Mom, but at school quite a few of the girls had nice clothes and I hated to run into them looking awful. The best-dressed girl, named Phyllis Miller, sat right in front of me. She had thirteen outfits, never wearing anything closer than two weeks apart. She had mostly plaid skirts with matching sweaters in shades of blue, green, tan, and red. She also had three jumpers and some wool jersey tops in pastel shades. Everything was the best material. She also had three tweed straight skirts, hard to tell apart. Once in a while she wore a bulky-knit white sweater over her different outfits. She also had two skirts that she wore once and I never saw again. The next two best-dressed girls, named Connie Barrone and Maureen Daly, had nine outfits each. Most of them were really beautiful, but some weren't too great. Connie had a gray gabardine skirt she wore quite often, probably so she wouldn't get tired of her other things. She had five very good coordinated outfits, skirts and matching sweaters or jerseys. There were some other girls with a few nice outfits. Sometimes I thought a certain girl (like Judy Dorhner) didn't have such a good wardrobe, and then she'd come in with two new outfits the same week. I was down at the bottom of the list. If I had the money I would have bought a royal blue wool jumper, two or three white long-sleeved blouses, a man-tailored shirt with a thin blue stripe, a maroon skirt to wear with a white sweater, a black and white plaid pleated wool skirt to wear with a long-sleeved red sweater, a black-watch plaid skirt to wear with a white or navy sweater, a gray wool straight skirt to wear with a light blue or light pink blouse, or with a white sweater, a bluish-purple jumper to wear with a white jersey or a light blue blouse, and a tan corduroy jumper to wear with a cocoa-brown sweater or white jersey. If I really had the money I'd probably just go to a good store like the Knitwear Shoppe and see things I never even thought of, although I'd try to look for that list.

Mom ran the washing machine now and then, but she didn't have any system for the laundry and it was usually in quite a mess. She just dumped piles of laundry in the closets and on the floor in the basement. When you went to look for anything you had to go through old shoes, winter clothes, straw hats, baby's snowsuits, and different outgrown things. She didn't know where anything was but usually she said it was in a certain pile. Many times I slept in tops from one pair of pajamas and bottoms from another because I couldn't find matches after looking through every pile in sight. Once I had three tops and couldn't find any bottoms. She told me they were in a pile in John's closet. I looked but all I could find was some long white underwear that once belonged to my grandfather. He brought it on a visit thinking it was freezing up north. Mom said why not wear them? I did, as I was at the end of my rope and wanted something warm, but I was so frustrated about all my pajamas being lost that I started crying with rage. I told her I didn't know how she managed to make such a mess out of everything. She laughed, saying I was quite a sight crying in her father's BVD's. To her we were all stuffed shirts, she had to keep kidding us so we wouldn't get too conceited. She put Dad's underwear in the washing machine with a red bathrobe and it came out pink. The next morning he discovered all his underwear was pink. To his annoyance he didn't have anything else to wear to work. He was afraid someone would see his underpants in the men's room. Mom said he had no sense of humor. According to her, as long as he didn't get into an accident he was safe. Celia had a bad experience with Mom. Mom threw out all her clothes for senior year, giving them to the Salvation Army even though they were brand new. Celia sewed them at home on the summer vacation to save money and kept them in the cedar chest, but when fall came she discovered they were gone. Mom casually said she was sorry.

I once played a good trick on my teacher in first grade, Miss Darien. She was always looking for kids chewing gum, which was unforgivable to her. She was strict, and quite a shock after kindergarten. She said bubble gum could ruin your vocal cords if you swallowed it. When she saw someone chewing, she asked him if he had gum in his mouth. When he denied it she grabbed him by the jaw so he couldn't swallow. Then she found the gum. I pretended to be quietly chewing gum, with no real gum in my mouth. It looked like I was chewing but trying to hide it. In a few minutes Miss Darien asked me if I was chewing gum and I said no. She quickly grabbed me and forced my mouth open, but naturally she couldn't find any gum as she expected. She let me go, I said, "I told you I wasn't chewing gum." What could she do but apologize.

Mom and Dad had another fight about money, Dad saying he could never get out of debt because of Mom's irresponsibility. He brought up the times she went back home, taking Celia, me, and the baby with her and leaving him alone in an empty house paying the bills. The trips were once a year (third, fourth, and fifth grade). We usually stayed about two months. When Mom decided to go, it started a long series of fights. Dad argued that she couldn't just take Celia and me out of school, leaving him alone with the house and dog, and spending hundreds of dollars which they didn't have. Mom said she had to see her father, brother, and old friends, and it would help her pull herself together. Dad didn't agree but finally Mom just said she was going and he'd better dig up the money somewhere. We took a compartment on "The

Southerner" leaving from Pennsylvania Station. Dad was furious and not saying a word. Celia cried, saying she'd stay home and cook for Dad, but neither one wanted her to. Mom just tried to ignore the gloom and kept chatting merrily like it was a bon voyage party. Fortunately she didn't drink on the train. We were on it two days and two nights and in close quarters. It cost a fortune to have meals in the dining car and even Mom was shocked about the prices—$5 or $6 for dinner. Celia suggested we have a big lunch and just pick up snacks for later, which we did the second day and saved quite a lot. Lunch came to about $2 each.

I was glad to get pulled out of school, but unfortunately I had to go to school in Virginia the first trip down there (third grade). I couldn't get used to the customs and didn't make any friends in the class as it was only for two months. I had a calendar of days until summer vacation and crossed off a day every night. Mom's cousin, named Shirley, was a top administrator of the Girl Scouts and Brownies there and wanted me to join the Brownies. I refused, and she and Mom both started picking on me, also telling the teacher in my class about it. The teacher, Miss Lemley, started talking to me one day after school for no reason (supposedly). When she brought up the Brownies I started running home. She ran after me across the playground and into the woods. I kept screaming, "no, no, no," really getting scared as she caught up with me and grabbed me. Finally I couldn't get my way and I went to two meetings and got the Brownie uniform. The first meeting we made hand puppets out of paper bags. We drew faces with crayons and glued yellow wool on the sides for hair. I put mine in braids. "Cousin Shirley" came by and I was surprised to see how much everyone respected her
58

(including the troop leader), as I always thought of her just as a friend of Mom's. She asked me how I was and how I liked the meeting. I had to ask her for a nickel for dues, as I didn't know about them and didn't have any money. She gave me a ride home. Mom was waiting and she and Shirley started talking about different people they knew. Mom played with the puppet, making it talk and making up a story. The second meeting of the Brownies was a field trip to the Richmond Zoo, where initiations were held. We were all supposed to learn a rhyme, spin around the wishing well with our eyes closed, and be initiated and receive the Brownie pin. I was in a panic when I heard the girls talking about the rhyme which everyone was practicing all week, as I couldn't remember anything about it even though I was present at the first meeting. Also I never heard anyone say "by heart" before so I was in the dark when one of the girls said we had to learn the rhyme "by heart." We had to say it separately as we were spun around by the troop leader. Luckily I was toward the end of the line so I had a chance to hear about ten girls say it. When my turn came I knew it almost by heart, just mumbling a few words I didn't know, which no one noticed. When I got home I ripped off my uniform and got into some play clothes. I didn't go to the next meeting and no one noticed. Then I was happy to hear the troop was letting out early for summer, and right after that we went home anyway. The next trip down, I begged not to enroll in the Richmond school. I offered to take my books along and cover all the ground I missed. Mom saw my teacher and the principal about it and they agreed. I was overjoyed. As usual, I didn't do the work every day, leaving it all to the end. Unfortunately, that was the only year (fourth grade) we

59

had geography, which I never learned. I hated to see the book sitting around and after a while the sight of it began to scare me and I was afraid to open it. When we got home I had to outline ten chapters in about three days before I could go back to school. My teacher, Mrs. Clark, wanted me to give an oral report on the southern United States, and I read the chapter in my book. I talked about the cotton crop, sugar cane, and sulfur mining in Louisiana. I also pointed out the Gulf Stream and the Mississippi River on the map, and the southern mountain ranges. She wanted me to give my personal opinion of the people, and I said they were the same but did everything slower, and had the best manners—all the children called their parents and teachers "sir" and "ma'am." No one would think of rough talk in the classroom. When I said that the class burst out laughing, thinking of Mrs. Clark, who used to be a sergeant in the WAC's and was always drilling us on the playground for punishment, and talking like the typical army sergeant, calling us "you brazen nitwits," etc.

"Poll" Greenleaf, an old friend of Mom's family from Texas, came to New York to see the Broadway shows and visited Mom. She owned oil land in Texas but lived in Virginia for the social life, where she became the best friend of Mom's mother. She always liked to see how Mom was doing. She was rolling in money with a mink coat, expensive perfume, false hair pieces, etc. She was about sixty-five but looked about thirty, with blond hair and no wrinkles on her face. She looked younger than Mom, or at least more glamorous. I was horrified when I found out she was coming to the house, as it was a horrible mess. I didn't know what she thought of Mom for living there. Mom didn't care. She didn't even clean up as she knew I'd race around doing it while she was out meeting "Poll" at her hotel. She got a lot of work out of me that way. I cleaned up the house in about five hours, getting the worst things straightened up. When Mom came back with "Poll" she told her I cleaned up the whole house saying didn't it look wonderful. Poll had grandchildren in private school who took music and dancing lessons in their spare time and never thought of doing housework, which was only for the maids, but she put on quite a show with Mom, saying I was an amazing little housekeeper. She brought a big box of candy, blue velvet dresses for Celia and me, and gave Mom a check for a hundred dollars, telling her to get herself a new suit. I was mortified that she saw what terrible shape we were all in, and I could have done without her loud comments on what a wonderful job I did on the house. I wanted to tell her I wasn't as stupid as she thought, I wasn't proud about doing a lot of dirty work, and I knew the house was ugly and the furniture was cheap, ugly, dirty, and about to fall apart. She said before we knew it I'd be making my debut. She drank a lot, but only the best, which she brought with her and was quite a treat for Mom and Dad. Poll said Dad was wonderful to pick up theater tickets for them, and he was so polite and handsome, the perfect gentleman. She asked me if I had a boyfriend and I said yes. She wanted to know if I could play the piano or a musical instrument and I told her no. I thought of telling her my method of getting stains out of rugs, just as a joke. She asked me if I was going to go to college and I said of course, looking at her like she must be crazy. She said I looked like Mom's mother, then changed her mind and said

61

Dad, then said Dad's mouth and nose, Mom's chin, etc. I had to model the velvet dress for them and she let me try on her mink coat, saying (with a big laugh) that I looked like the "mink type." I got the wild idea of asking her for money to fix up the house and get me a new wardrobe but naturally I didn't.

Poll and Mom discussed Mom's side of the family. I always hated to hear about the relatives, as it was always bad news. I had never even seen most of them even though we were the same flesh and blood and probably all resembled each other. Mom asked about "Cousin Lester." Poll said he still had a little drinking problem (that meant he was a terrible alcoholic, a doctor too). Mom brought up our cousin Lorraine, asking how she was getting along with her two sons since her husband Roger shot himself in the head (three years ago). It was the same story. Actually some of the relatives were doing nothing, moving, their children moving or graduating from college, everything normal, but with some of them everything was out of control.

Poll's grandson, Winfield, joined her in New York with his mother. He was on Easter vacation from military school and flew up for the week. The Greenleafs took Mom and me to see the Broadway show *Top Banana*. It was about a comedian in burlesque who wanted to be the top TV comedy star. There were a lot of chorus girls, different costumes, and dancing. One girl had a red sequin bra with little propellers on them which the comedian started spinning every time he walked by her, which got a lot of laughs.

Winfield wore his uniform and had the best manners, holding all the doors, getting orange drinks for everyone, etc. He had a terrific posture. After the show Poll suggested we go to see the lights of

Broadway and Times Square so we got into a cab and drove around. Poll said we could go see any of the sights of New York and I suggested 92nd Street. I'd seen the movie called *The House on 92nd Street* and I wanted to see if it was really in New York. Poll agreed and the cabdriver whizzed up to 92nd and drove slowly along the street. A lot of houses looked alike over there and I couldn't tell if we were passing the house in the movie on those dark streets. The cabdriver thought it was a stupid idea and said why not go to Chinatown, but Poll said she wanted to take us out to eat so we went to the Taft Grill. Vincent Lopez was there with his dance band, making special dedications to people with birthdays and anniversaries. I wore my velvet dress and Mom wore a new black suit. She looked quite nice but her hair wasn't too good. She was thin from drinking, but she looked prettier than Poll or Winfield's mother, who were on the fat side in spite of their drinking. I guess they didn't cut down on food like Mom. Poll kept saying the show was "just darlin'." In the ladies' room Mom told me she thought the show stank. She said we should go to a serious play some time, not the kind Poll liked. According to her Poll was drunk all the time although it didn't show and couldn't follow a plot— that was why she only went to musicals.

At the table all the adults had drinks. They talked about old times, about Winfield's and his sister Gloria Lynn's private schools, and Poll said Mom should come back home as she could see New York didn't agree with her. Mom said maybe she would. I said, not thinking, but just to say something, that things were the same everywhere and everyone laughed. I had a steak sandwich. I suddenly discovered I left my program in the ladies' room and ran to get it. It was on the couch in front of the mirror. I sat down to relax a minute away from everything. In the mirror I looked quite nice, about eighteen or nineteen. I wished I was there on my anniversary. I went back to the table and we stayed quite a while. Mom and I took the last bus home from the Port Authority. She didn't act drunk although she'd been drinking with them all night. She said Poll was no great brain but she had a lot of money. Poll's adopted son, Winfield, once proposed to Mom, but he lost an arm in army training. Mom said she never thought of marrying him after that, saying it would have been false charity, and she fell in love with Dad, who was athletic and all in one piece. She said I could probably marry Winfield, Jr. if I wanted to, although we didn't hit it off too well and he had a girl friend back home. Mom said she didn't regret not marrying Winfield Greenleaf and living down there, because the brand of liquor she drank didn't matter that much to her. She stared out the window a while and then fell asleep. I watched out for our stop and woke her up when we got to our corner.

When Celia went off to college I couldn't get used to having a big bed to roll around in. Mom used to say I needed a bed of my own but we never got around to getting one. I didn't mind as Celia and I didn't get into fights, she didn't snore or take all the room, etc. When she was in high school she stayed up late reading or doing homework but the light was low and I fell right asleep. We used to pretend we were watching TV before we really had one. On the wall across from our bed the street light came in through the window. It made a big square on the wall, just like a TV in the dark.

Then the shadows of leaves came in, always moving around, just like programs. It was practically as good as a real television. A couple of nights we stayed up watching it, pretending it was boxing matches and different programs. I never got used to a bed of my own so I didn't even want one. Once Mom went to the hospital for a few days and Dad had to leave on a business trip. Then we had room to spread out all over the house but we didn't even bother. Celia and I got the house in terrific shape and there was a lot of peace and quiet. She told Johnnie stories every night, cleaned up his room and made his bed, trimmed his hair, etc., as she really loved him. She always wanted him to get to bed before eight but we stayed up to all hours since it was summer and no school. She and I cooked a lot for the three of us and discovered a terrific way to make eggs. Scramble four eggs, add one tablespoon of milk, ½ teaspoon of salt, and dash of pepper. Add ¼ teaspoon of dry mustard and one tablespoon of finely chopped onion. Slice one slice of American cheese into very small squares, cutting crisscross. Heat skillet and melt one tablespoon of butter in it, pour in eggs. After eggs are heated up but not cooked too much, drop in pieces of cheese. Scramble the usual way.

I stayed up late reading *Champion's Choice* in bed. When I turned out the light the moonbeams were coming in the room through the window. I took a look out the window—all the houses on the street looked quiet, and no one was around, with the street lights shining through the trees. I had the crazy idea something was calling me to go outside but I just tried to toss it off as I got in bed. I couldn't fall asleep, I had the idea of running over to the sandpit and throwing all my money in the woods over there. If Celia was still home I would have waked her up, hoping she'd talk me out of it, but it was no use waking up Mom. I put my dungarees over my pajamas, plus loafers and my pea jacket, and got my owl bank out of the bureau. I had to tiptoe slowly down our creaking staircase so I wouldn't wake up the family. When I got outside in the moonlight I felt like it was a good idea but I didn't want to run into anyone as they'd wonder what I was up to. I walked down Morgan over to Chestnut, which was a dead end with a fence blocking it off. Over that was a hill rolling down, and at the bottom no fields but some new houses on a winding road—all wood houses with no paint yet. It looked quiet as there were street lights, no trees, and no people, just empty houses. It was part of a new dvelopment I forgot about. I had to go over to Kruger where there were still some fields. Down past Kruger I saw a clump of grass as high as my head with some tiger lilies poking out of it. They were the only color, orange. I threw my money in there. I couldn't get the bottom out of the bank so I had to crack it on the ground—it was plaster. I had mostly nickels, dimes, and pennies, coming to about $2.50. I threw a few handfuls which fell quietly in the grass. Then I started running, suddenly remembering there might be snakes around. I got back to Chestnut and headed home, but as I got to the corner a car turned in from Kruger and shined its headlights on me. It was the police, wondering what I was doing on the streets so late, and asking where I lived. I said I had to see my aunt on Chestnut and now I was heading home. They said to get in, they'd give me a lift. I agreed. They asked me what my aunt's name was. I said the first name I thought of, "Mrs. Fields," as

I was just running in the fields. They didn't know anyone with that name, but naturally they didn't know everyone in town. It was two policemen in the front and me in the back seat. I asked them if they knew Henny, the cop who directed traffic in front of the school—they did. In about two minutes we were at my house. They waited till I got in the door and took off without making much noise, so no one woke up. I tiptoed in my room, got undressed and crawled into bed, falling asleep right away.

We had cockroaches, thanks to Mom's housekeeping. They were mostly in the kitchen. I probably ate plenty of things that cockroaches ran over, without knowing it (or wanting to know). We had a few campaigns to get rid of them when it was getting impossible. Dad used JO paste spread on pieces of potato. It had a terrible smell, especially if you knew what it was for. Mom hated it when he put it out. I did too, although I wanted to get rid of the "bugs," as we called them. I thought Dad didn't really care about getting rid of them—he just liked to spread the paste and set the potato all over the place when he was really drunk and taking a break from sports. Once in a while I beat him to the punch and went on a big campaign to get rid of every last cockroach. I had the all-or-nothing attitude. Dad just put out some paste and didn't care where they went to die, but I wanted to get them all down to the last male and female so they couldn't come back. It was ridiculous to try to kill them one at a time, as it wasn't even a drop in the bucket. It made me feel like a fool to run around just to hit one little bug.

My plan was to cover all areas of the house and

keep all food in the refrigerator. I washed the outside of all jars, closing all food packages on the shelves tightly and throwing out anything that looked suspicious. I cleaned the most obvious places, like the grease on the stove, which they fed on. They were attracted to anything greasy, including the oil inside the clock. I saw quite a few run in and out of there a few times. I used JO all over the place, mostly in the kitchen, but also the bathroom, dining room, and basement. After two days I vacuumed and swept all over, getting a big pile of them from behind the refrigerator. I repeated this after four days, following with another sweeping. I did "light" tests, coming into the kitchen when it was completely dark for a couple of hours and suddenly turning on the lights. This used to show thousands of cockroaches running to hide. After the first day of my plan I saw a lot less, about twenty-five. After a week there were only three. Then I just used spray. Finally I could go into the bathroom or kitchen at any time of night, turn on the light, open a drawer, and not see one. Then I took everything off the shelves, washed them down with Spic and Span and then did a rinse with a stiff solution of Clorox. I sprayed all around the baseboards and in any corners or cracks. I thought if there were any babies waiting to hatch in a few days they couldn't survive in that atmosphere. I once saw about ten tiny ones hatch. They came out of a little tan capsule that the mother carried along until it got too heavy and dropped. The babies came out very small when the capsule sort of flaked away, running in all directions—black with little white spots on the head. They must have grown to full size in a matter of days, as I saw ones that little only once in a blue moon. I thought of putting a little one in a jar to see how long it would take to grow into the kind I saw all over the place, but never did. I could have given a science report on them for Miss DePauw, bringing in samples of the broken egg, a tiny one, a pregnant female with the egg developing, a middle-sized one, and then the adult, but it would have been too embarrassing. When I swept out behind the refrigerator I found a big one that was pure white—exactly like the others in every way except color. It gave me quite a shock and I thought of saving it as it might be quite valuable. I had seen so many for so many years and never an albino. Even the little feelers in front were white. I showed it to Mom and Dad but then threw it out. After that complete clean-out, the place stayed free of bugs for quite a while. Mom was glad when they were gone but didn't really care one way or the other, and wouldn't follow my kitchen rules, as her way of defying me.

I went to the movies with Lois Saturday. We saw *Kid Galahad* and *Room for One More* at the Fox, and had sodas after. We stopped at the library and I took out *Thunderbolt House* and *No Pattern for Love*. On my way home, I practically fainted when I saw my house. The baby was leaning out the front window of my bedroom, I could see him halfway down the block. I didn't yell as I was afraid he'd start talking back to me and forget where he was and fall. I ran behind the Bundys' and came in my house through the back, praying he wouldn't be dead on the ground when I got upstairs. On the stairs I practically trampled him as he came running down. It turned out he was doing an "experiment"—filling Coke bottles with water, dropping them out the window, running

69

down to get them, bringing them up again, dropping them out the window again, and so on. He thought he knew what he was doing. Mom didn't keep an eye on him so he thought he was as old as anyone else and did whatever he felt like. He started crying and kicked me in the leg. I yelled at him saying it was dangerous to play by windows but I don't know if it made any impression on him.

On the weekends Dad could be impossible, as he started drinking early and watched the ball games on TV. By the time the games were over, he was in a nasty mood. He loved to watch me work. I got out of the house whenever possible on weekends, going to the movies or just hanging around with some of the kids in the neighborhood, mostly to get away from Dad. Mom slept most of the day. It was really her usual sleeping schedule but it seemed different on the weekends.

One Saturday I was out all day and came in when it got dark. Dad was waiting for me and gave me a real look of hatred when I came in the kitchen, saying, "And just what have *you* done today?" I said I was out with Lois and some kids and he gave me a nasty look, saying, "Just look at this kitchen." The kitchen was a mess, with dishes and food and dirty clothes all over the place. Out of fear, I said I'd clean it up. I took the laundry down to the basement and started a white wash of Dad's and John's underwear, plus some towels. Then I stacked the dishes and put the food, jars, etc., away. The trouble with the house was you could never stop once you got started. As soon as you opened the refrigerator you discovered it needed cleaning and you were off for another hour's job—the same for the stove and cupboards. I did a very thorough job to appease Dad. I had nothing to do that night anyway. I had two history chapters to read and about fifty questions to answer at the end, but I knew I was probably going to leave it for Sunday anyway. Dad left me alone in the kitchen and about 11 o'clock when I was at last getting to the floor, he came in. He was drunker than ever but not mad at me as he could see I was slaving away. I was hoping Mom might wake up. He leaned against the wall and stared at me scrubbing, saying what a great job I was doing, and what a terrific difference between the clean and dirty sides of the floor, expecting me to get all excited about it. I didn't say anything to him, waiting for him to get out. He hung around smiling and I realized he was planning to stay. I told him would he please get out, not really yelling as I was afraid he might hit me. I was afraid of him when he was drunk, not like Mom who I always thought I could handle physically. He said didn't I like the company? I said I didn't like to be stared at when I was working. He reluctantly left, going out to the living room. A little later he came back, raving about the floor some more, and got a glass of milk and a big bowl of ice cream. The bowl he always used was big with high sides. It looked like a dog-food bowl to me and always got on my nerves.

A couple of summers we went to visit Mom's relatives. I had an old Aunt Sally, really Mom's aunt, who lived in Atlanta with her mother, my great-grandmother. My great-grandmother, who we called Nonny, was eighty-nine. Aunt Sally was seventy-one but acted much younger. She was always fetching and running around for her mother, and Nonny told everyone how incompetent Sally was.

It was torture to stay in the same room with Nonny. She was a mass of wrinkles and sat in a wheelchair all day. She had a cracked voice you could hardly understand. It didn't sound human. She kept saying she couldn't give us very much but she gave us a name we could be proud of. I would have made myself a laughing stock saying that in New Jersey, but naturally Celia and I just acted like we were profoundly impressed by everything she said. I didn't like her but Dad said I should spend more time talking to her (listening to her) and it was too bad if I wasn't interested or if the room put me in a terrible state of gloom. When Nonny showed you her china or silver or even gave you a piece of candy, she tried to make you think it was the best in the world and you should practically fall down and worship it. She didn't care about Celia or John or me or how we did in school, or how Mom and Dad were getting along. She kept talking about the wonderful family name she gave us, as though a big estate went with it and Dad didn't have to shake in his shoes about getting a raise. She said we should be proud of our great family traditions above all. To Dad the idea that someone bored or depressed me meant nothing. He believed in respecting your elders. He wanted me to do my duty by her, letting her hug me (because of her great love for me supposedly) until I died of suffocation as far as he was concerned.

Nonny and Aunt Sally lived on a side street off one of the main streets in Atlanta. The house was big but very cramped inside. This was because they brought all their furniture from their old house, a mansion according to them, to this one, and had boarders upstairs. The furniture and china all over the place made it look like an old furniture store.

Aunt Sally kowtowed to her mother all her life and even at her age was always saying, "Yes, Mama, yes, Mama, yes, Mama," as she ran around. She was much nicer than her mother. Even though she never got married or got out from under Nonny's thumb, she was surprisingly good-natured and had a cheerful attitude about life. That horrible environment didn't have any effect on her (I could see Mom drinking herself blind to blot it out). It was a complete mystery to me.

Being in that house with them made me very depressed and we had to stay a week. They had no TV and the only thing on the radio was hillbilly music. Celia was in a terrible mood and always reading. Mom and Dad stayed sober during the day and sneaked drinks at night. Finally Aunt Sally said she wanted to treat me and Celia to a picture show. I was overjoyed. There was a movie theater just a couple of blocks away, which we'd have never guessed. When we got there the smell of popcorn and the carpet in the lobby and the posters of coming attractions took a big load off my mind. I felt a million times better and all my worries seemed to go away. The movie was a comedy set in a hotel in the Middle East, *Hotel Sahara*. Celia and I cracked up over it. Aunt Sally couldn't follow the movie. She looked at us in wonder when we laughed, and then sometimes she tried to join in to be friendly, but always looking at us instead of the movie. Finally she said she'd better get home and she'd see us after the show to treat us to ice cream. In about an hour she came back, not realizing it was a double feature, and left again after fifteen minutes, this time for good. The second one was *Clash by Night*. Movies didn't mean anything to her. All she said while she watched was, "Well, I declare."

One of their boarders was an old man named Mr. Tripp who had an old car he kept in their driveway. He was always polishing it. There was a swing on the front porch that Aunt Sally swang on in the evenings. Mr. Tripp used to sit with her sometimes but Nonny started making fun of "Sally's boyfriend" to everyone, so Aunt Sally avoided him, feeling quite embarrassed. Of course Nonny also said Mr. Tripp was incredibly common compared to her, and it was ridiculous to think of him talking to her daughter.

When we were in the car driving away from Atlanta, Mom sang a song saying it was an old English ballad.

> *My grandmammy and old Aunt Sally*
> *Both live together on shinny-bone alley.*
> *With a number on the gate and a sign on the door*
> *They both live over the grocery store.*

I told Mom never to sing it again—I hated the sound of it. It sounded to me like the kind of song a crazy person would sing behind a wall, trying to drive me crazy wondering where it came from. She said "for God's sakes," very disgustedly. It reminded me of how poor Nonny and Aunt Sally were, in spite of Nonny's great airs. I hated to think of my relatives like that. It was like two poor old ladies living in a back alley, with skinny ankles and nothing to eat except some canned things from the grocery downstairs which they could hardly pay for.

Once Aunt Sally took me upstairs to show me a "pineapple" bed, with removable bedpost tops. The bedposts were hollow and carved like pineapples piled on top of each other. She whispered to me like it was still a big secret, "This is where we hid the silver when the Yankees came." The other boarder was a lady who lived in the room with that bed. She was a career girl. She had a lot of knick-knacks and gave me a miniature bottle of Coca-cola to play with.

Celia and I were always saying we'd never go down to Texas to see Granny again. Her big dog-house got on my nerves. It was a regular house behind her own house, with windows, doors, curtains, etc., but for dogs. Granny raised cocker spaniels and showed them in the dog shows. Each dog had her own room, with rugs and furniture, everything exactly like a regular bedroom but with a box instead of a bed. The doors were different too, with flaps at the bottom. You could see dogs suddenly coming through the doors.

When we were down in Texas, Mom or Dad always insisted on taking me and Celia to a swimming pool in another town, about a forty-minute drive from Granny's. One day Celia had a cold and was spending all day in bed sleeping so I went alone. Mom drove me. She was drinking but supposedly not too much so Granny wouldn't notice. She and Dad both drank there, keeping a bottle in the room, but Mom worse than Dad. We always wished she wouldn't with Granny against her. Once Granny tried to start a conversation with me asking how would I like a nice house, a car when I was seventeen, new clothes, etc., meaning how would I like her and Dad to take over and get rid of Mom. Celia and I were loyal to Mom. Granny never drank and she was always in the same cheerful mood but she had a terrible personality, bossy, hypocritical, always treating Dad like the stupid baby and humiliating him in front of people, thinking of herself as the great beauty queen (going around barefoot) even though she was fat, weighing about 200 pounds. (She was short too.) She loved to eat and cook and was always making us big dinners, to fatten us up as she would say, but I lost my appetite. She was so proud to have a big freezer with a year's supply of frozen food.

At the swimming pool I met a boy (about 11) who was a terrific diver. He could do swan dives and jackknifes off the ten-foot board. His name was Peter. He was an Indian, with straight black hair, but just looked like he had a terrific tan. He went to a regular school, not on a reservation. There were a lot of Indians down there and none in New Jersey. He taught me how to do a plain dive from the edge of the pool. He was surprised I could swim fast and challenged me to a race, which he won. The time really flew with him showing me how to swim under water and find money at the bottom of the pool. It helped me get over my fear of the water. I found a quarter and a nickel and he found nothing so I got him an ice cream. Mom was supposed to pick me up at 4:00 so I had to leave and get dressed. I felt good although my eyes were stinging from the chlorine. I saw Pete playing with some other kids. I had to wait for Mom in the parking lot but I could see the pool through the wire fence. I hated waiting alone, plus after an hour of waiting I was furious that I got out of the pool early for nothing. Then I got scared that something had happened to Mom. I kept looking down the highway thinking I saw her but each time it turned out to be just another car. Remembering her reckless driving I began to think she had had an accident and was never going to come. Then the swimming pool closed (at 6:00) and all the kids came out. Pete saw me and said, "Are you still here?" really surprised. I decided to call home although the call was 10¢ and I only had a nickel. The girl wanted to close up and told me to get along but I started crying, telling her I had to make the call, so she agreed and gave me a nickel. I had to get Granny's number from information. I kept thinking of getting the news Mom was dead, I could hardly stop crying. Dad answered the phone and I started crying again when I heard his voice. He thought something had happened to me at the pool. I said I'd been waiting for two hours and where was Mom? He said she was all right and had just left. He was disgusted with me for crying and said she'd be right there. I was relieved but felt furious about all the worry and waiting. About 7:00 Mom finally drove up, with the parking lot empty and everybody gone home. I was still worried as I didn't know how I'd call home if she didn't come and it was getting dark fast. She was still drunk, not too different from the morning. She didn't even know she was late. I told her I was worried sick and she apologized but didn't really care. I started crying again, she got disgusted saying it was all my imagination that she was in an accident.

When we got home I didn't want to see Granny and Dad, but Celia was awake in bed reading. I had dinner on a tray in her room although Granny called me a spoiled brat. I told Celia the whole story and started crying all over again. She said Mom was fighting all day with Granny and Dad and got raging drunk in the middle of the day, but was sobered up a little now. Granny criticized her drinking, her spending Dad's money, and her bringing up Celia and me with no discipline. She said Mom thought she was from the best people but she wasn't worth a dime. She said Mom's family was on the skids and had no money. Mom didn't answer and Dad just stood on the side. Mom said she'd never let her children go to Dad and Granny. Mom accused Granny of being a religious hypocrite. (She was.) Granny said we'd soon realize where we were better off but Mom said we'd never agree. Celia said the fighting went on all day. That's why they always tried to get us out to the pool, so they could discuss plans for a divorce. Her cold was better. I was really miserable with all of Mom's and Dad's drinking down there. It was even worse with Granny around watching it all and trying to get into the act. We couldn't stand it around the house so we went swimming every day. Mom or Dad drove us over. I was always afraid to come home, thinking something awful had happened while we were away. Their different plans for a divorce never worked out. I couldn't stand the meals. I used to long for them to go to bed early so I could watch television or just fool around with Celia. I read a lot of library books and played with the dogs, but sometimes I couldn't get interested in anything.

I didn't like long trips in the car with the family because then the problem of eating came up with Dad. At home Mom called up her friend Roger at the grocery every day and ordered food so there was always something around the house and I was never hungry, but on family trips all the food had to come out of Dad's pocket. I never had enough to eat. Dad always acted flabbergasted at the price of hamburgers, soda, ice cream, etc.—everything except beer and whiskey. I used to ask for all I wanted, but after a while his groaning and sighing got on my nerves and my pride couldn't take it.

On the way home from Texas we stopped at a drive-in hamburger stand about six o'clock at night. I breathed a sigh of relief when Dad turned off the road because I had been hungry since noon. Fortunately Mom picked up a bag of potato chips for me when she was in a little store getting beer. I could have always asked them to stop and eat and they would have done it but I couldn't stand Dad's disgusted look. I ordered a hamburger and when it came I ate it like a wild beast. I was dying for another one and hoping Mom would go out and get more of her own accord, but she never had a big appetite. Dad turned around with a big sigh, saying, "Is that enough?" I said yes and looked out the window, not wanting to talk to him. Dad asked Mom how much it came to and she carelessly said a couple of dollars. He whistled and said, "My god!" Mom said, "You're a big boy now, Harry—you know prices are always going up." Dad said, "They seem to be" under his breath. Mom opened a can of beer and started staring out the window with a disgusted look, not answering him. He always acted surprised about the cost of living. Once I had to ask him for money for shoes and he said, "Will two dollars be enough?" I started to say yes and take it, thinking I'd forget about worrying until I got to the shoe store. I just wanted to get away from him. I thought he didn't know anything about prices and lived in a dream world, then I remembered he had to pass stores in New York every day on the way to work. I told him I'd never heard of shoes for that. The best I could do was $3.98 at National or Miles. I said if he knew where I could get shoes for $2.00 he should tell me and I'd go. He said all right very disgustedly, giving me two more. One time I was out with my Uncle Tyler and two cousins and we stopped at a diner. We all had hamburgers and when we finished he asked us all if we wanted more. I said no, well trained by Dad. He insisted, saying one wasn't enough for a good lunch, and I agreed. He said he could hear my stomach growling and laughed. I felt terrific. When we got up from the table I got dizzy and almost fell on the floor. Everyone laughed, including me. He was my only uncle. Unfortunately he lived in Virginia and only visited us once in New Jersey. I felt terrific when he was around, just the opposite of how I felt with Dad. It was far less nerve-racking to get money from Mom. I hated to argue with Dad and usually I just stupidly said yes when he asked me if a couple of dollars would be enough to buy a dress or shoes, or ten for a winter coat. Mom bought a bag of popcorn which she said I should hold onto in case I got hungry later. I ate it right away and was pretty full. She also passed around a bottle of Coke which I took a few big swallows of.

I had a couple of library books along, and I read some of *Mountain Laurel*. Reading in the car always gave me a headache after a while, so I had to stop and just look at the scenery. Dad was trying to make four or five hundred miles a day so we drove until late with some of us dozing off. Mom fell asleep. We waited too long to find a motel and there were "no vacancy" signs all over the place. Finally Dad pulled up at a place that didn't have a sign and went into the office. Mom woke up while he was in there. She was drunk, not just from beer but from a bottle of whiskey they kept on the floor in front, and she hadn't slept it off yet. She was more drunk when she woke up than when she fell asleep. She wanted to know what was going on.

80

Dad came back and disgustedly said there were no vacancies. It was around midnight. Mom didn't believe him. It was a modern motel and she thought there was a vacancy but Dad wouldn't pay the prices. Dad denied it but Mom was convinced he was lying and started calling him a cheapskate. She said she couldn't stand living with him any more. She made quite a scene and if there was anything I couldn't stand it was them fighting and yelling in the car with me about two feet away. Dad said it wasn't the money and he'd pay anything for a room as he was ready to drop. Mom didn't believe him, insisting on going in to check with the manager. When she came back she was still furious even though she found out Dad was telling the truth. She kept insulting him and said she couldn't stand living with such a miserable tightwad. She had a couple more drinks and kept yelling at him as we drove along looking for another place. He said, "Haven't you had enough?" and she said, "Not on your sweet life," taking another swig. Celia was crying in the corner all wrapped up in a blanket, shaking like a leaf. Finally we found a place with a big double room for sixteen dollars. The next night Dad started looking earlier and we found a terrific place in Illinois. It was a group of log cabins spread out over a wood, each named after a president. We got the "Andrew Jackson." The cabin was nice and clean, old-fashioned but with a nice bathroom. The big surprise was it was incredibly cheap—only $2.00 a night. The owner must not have cared about money. I was happy for Dad and relieved about not having to listen to him complain. He acted like it was a pretty good price, but still high. I told him it was a steal and he nodded his head but looked away like he was thinking about something else.

I read *Lantern in Her Hand*. It was set in the old days, about a girl who married a man who went West. She gave up her life in the East and worked like a dog all her life, keeping their log cabin clean, using oiled paper for glass in the windows, making her own soap and candles, even learning to shoot because of wildcats and snakes. She ruined her hands, which she was always proud of, and began to look old in a few years. She had five children, giving birth in the cabin each time with only a midwife there. She didn't see anyone for weeks at a time and had to teach the children to read and write as there were no schools. Her husband died and the children grew up. They went back East to live, becoming successful doctors, businessmen, and teachers. They tried to persuade her to move back and lead an easier life but she refused. They thought she was hopelessly old-fashioned, laughing at the way she wore her hair, etc.

I won a contest for an essay on Dad! It was a newspaper contest for Father's Day held by *Our Town* (for three towns). I entered thinking it would be a surprise for the family but I never expected to win. I wrote about all the good things about Dad—that he was patient, taught me to obey the rules and do my schoolwork, didn't believe in hitting, worked hard, was down to earth, looked out for the family, and looked out for us all. There was a little headline in the paper, "Local Girl Writes Prizewinning Essay." They had my name and address and a couple of sentences from the essay. The prize was $10 and a free dinner for the whole family at Nystrom's Restaurant on route 17. Dad was pretty surprised when he heard. I was nervous that they'd have a photographer there as we went in but they didn't and we had a pretty good time—Celia, me, the baby, and Mom and Dad. Celia was in a good mood and laughed all day. In the ladies' room she said the idea of me winning the contest almost made her hysterical. She meant since I didn't get along with Dad and wouldn't watch TV if he was in the same room. We had a terrific dinner and I had coffee afterwards with Celia and my parents.

Mom decided to get a teacher's license so she could start teaching in the elementary school near our house. She brought it up with Dad, saying it would get her out of the house, let her use her college education, and the few extra thousand a year would make all the difference in the family income. Once she started, she could afford a part-time cleaning lady. They could clear up their debts, save some money, and in about a year buy a house in Englewood or Tenafly and start associating with a better class of people. They wanted to move since none of the neighbors had gone to college and had worse jobs than Dad. It was a mystery why our house was still the eyesore of the block, but it was the old story of how we didn't economize. Dad didn't like the idea of Mom teaching, just wanting her to do a better job at home. He said he was the old-fashioned type who thought a woman's place was in the home, but he finally agreed, probably thinking anything was worth a try to stop her drinking.

To get a license, Mom had to take four education courses at Paterson State or Montclair Teacher's College, which she could do in a year, going to night school twice a week. She registered at Montclair as it was closer. Classes were twice a week, Tuesday and Thursday. She didn't drink for a couple of days to get ready for the first class. She got more nervous the closer it came but left in pretty good spirits. When she got home she was excited and gay, saying she'd had a great time. She asked questions in class, and after the bell rang the professor took her aside, saying he was glad to have someone so interested as a student. She told him about her getting an M.A. in English but never being able to use her education after she got married. I couldn't get used to the idea of Mom being in school, with books and homework. She had a big textbook, *Principles of Primary Education*, which she said looked like a breeze. According to her, it wasn't the kind of course you had to study for—just show up and throw the bull in class discussion. Unfortunately, she started drinking again Thursday. She denied it and acted like nothing was wrong and she was going to go, but Celia persuaded her it was better to just miss the class than show up drunk. Celia said why not forget it this time and pull herself together for the next one. She gave her a long pep talk, suggesting that each night when Mom came home from class, Celia could have tea and a snack ready, and they could get together and do any homework Mom had for the next class so it wouldn't hang over her head. Celia said they could go in the dining room, she could do her own homework, and be there to help Mom out in case she felt rusty about schoolwork. Mom agreed but two days later she was drinking again and we all knew she couldn't go to the third class. She said she was going, denying drinking, but Celia blew up at her, telling her she didn't fool people as much as she thought. She yelled at her, saying what was the matter with her?—was she trying to destroy herself and never do anything worthwhile? What was she afraid of? They were only people in the class. Mom broke down crying, saying she just couldn't do it. She said all the years of living with Dad had destroyed her self-confidence. Celia was very discouraged about the whole thing as she had had her hopes up. She was telling me she thought this was "it" for Mom. Dad threw it up at Mom a few times after that, saying that was $90 down the drain for tuition, but Mom just shut him up, saying it was too damn bad about the money and she wasn't going to do anything she didn't want to do. She said if she was a little dumber, like him, she'd make out better in this world. Dad said we were lucky he wasn't like her.

Dad took me to Sears-Roebuck to get Mom a Christmas present. He was drunk and in an awful mood, and I was afraid to say no. They had just had a big fight. He bought her a garbage can, the small white kind for the kitchen with a step-on pedal to open the lid. As Mom's birthday was a few days before Christmas he also bought a mop. I always hated that store anyway as I had bought quite a few ugly things there, but it was the last straw to be trapped there with Dad. I wanted to wait in the car but he dragged me along to the kitchen sections. He looked at all the different garbage cans, asking for my opinion. He was quiet in public so I wasn't worried about him making a scene but I was nervous and said they were all nice. I felt mortified because I thought the lady knew it was for a Christmas present, and I finally walked away from him and looked at the model bathrooms until he decided. When we got home, Dad tried to pass off the presents as from both of us. Mom had taken a nap and was pretty sober.

When she saw the presents she was quite sarcastic and laughed at Dad, saying, "Oh, how lovely! Only you could think of this, Harry! I can hardly wait to try them on!" Dad didn't know what to say and went for a drive in the car. He came back in a worse mood than ever, but fortunately he was sleepy and went upstairs to bed. I felt like a big menace was out of the way with him asleep as I was afraid he was going to explode and hit me any minute.

We had the usual tree for Christmas. I never liked to help the family trim it, but since Dad was out of the way and Mom was resting, I started to do it by myself and had a good time. Celia came home from ice skating and helped me finish up. She brought a cake with her for Mom's birthday. Mom sat on the couch watching us hang the tinsel, putting the garbage can and mop under the tree as a joke. We had the cake and tea, and Mom acted quite sentimental about Celia remembering her birthday. I told her my Christmas present to her was under the tree. I asked Mom how old she was and she said she didn't know, Dad was thirty-nine and she thought she was a year younger.

Celia and I got velvet hats from "Poll" Greenleaf. Mine was red and hers was green, and they were both quite strange looking, with a gold ring at the back and a velvet flap going through like a ponytail. At first we didn't have the nerve to wear them to church, but finally we decided they were Christmas colors and we would be together. Also the church would be dark as it was the midnight Christmas Eve service. When we went up for communion, Tommy Everett (he was an altar boy and in my class at Somerset) started breaking up when he saw my hat. Celia and I could hardly keep from laughing and we tried not to look at him. They

86

sang Christmas carols, which gave me the Christmas spirit. I was happy to be out of the house. The church was trimmed all over with pine boughs and smelled just like the forest. Tommy's mother asked Mom, Celia, and me over to her house for eggnog, and we went. I talked to Tommy about all the homework we got over the vacation and he suggested we do half of the big history project each and then exchange. I always felt funny when I talked to someone from school outside of school, as if I thought everyone in my class lived together except me. He asked me where I got my hat and I said it was a present from a friend of the family. Mrs. Everett gave us some fruitcake which she said she made. The eggnog was spiked but Mom just drank a little and talked nicely to Mrs. Everett about the service and about Celia's college.

We didn't exchange too many big presents on Christmas, although the baby got quite a few toys. The year before Dad bought a ping-pong table as a gift to the whole family. Sometimes Celia and I went on a spree of playing and played for a whole day, especially if it was rainy out. I got pretty good with all the practice. Mom once drunkenly challenged me to a game. I thought I could easily beat her since she was unsteady on her feet but she won about 21 to 5. She said ping-pong was a cinch after tennis and she could beat me blindfolded. She wanted to tie a handkerchief across her eyes to play me again, saying she could tell by the sound where the ball was. She knew how to "cut" the ball so it was spinning when it hit my paddle, and I could never tell which way it was going to go.

Maureen Daly and Glamorene Parks saw me with Dad at Sears without me knowing. They told me in school, saying I had a cute father. I was afraid they saw us getting the garbage can but it was in the parking lot. Whenever the girls in my class saw him they were surprised anyone could have a father like that. I agreed as Dad was the typical athlete in looks—tall, dark, with brown eyes and a nice face.

I felt ambitious in the morning and wrote all my thank-you letters including one to Granny thanking her for the Christmas check she sent me ($5). I must have still had the Christmas spirit as I made it a long one saying I had a wonderful time in Texas every summer.

We got a surprise present from my grandfather in the mail—sugarcane. It looked like pieces of bamboo but you could chew on it and it was incredibly sweet. I could hardly believe that's where sugar comes from. Mom said when she was growing up she and her friends chewed it instead of gum. Her father's brother had a farm in Georgia and that's where he got it. We never heard from Granddad. Mom said he didn't have enough money to send presents so he never got in touch except once in a blue moon. Just for old times' sake I kept a little piece so I wouldn't forget what it was like.

Mom said she drove past the new modern church they built at Sacred Heart and it practically made her swear off drinking as she thought she had delirium tremens. This church had a glass tower you could see inside of and instead of the usual cross they had a crucifix of Jesus with a red heart. At night it glowed (that's when Mom saw it). It didn't look too religious, more like a valentine.

Mom said she was glad to be Episcopalian as it was the real American church without the hillbillies. So was I (thinking it gave me a purpose in life) although if she hadn't told me I never would have guessed, since St. Paul's was poor, small, and almost a shack. Thank God Granny and Dad didn't suck me into their religion, Baptist, but Dad wasn't religious and didn't care. St. Paul's only had seats for about 150 but that was more than enough. They couldn't afford to pay someone to clean it so Mrs. Lanford had to do it. (She always kept it clean.) It was good inside with stained glass windows, white walls, and dark wood for beams and ceiling, but looked worse outside. Sometimes the grass wasn't cut outside and Rev. Lanford acted strange at times, telling people how his wife hadn't bought a new dress for five years. He was heartbroken since the Catholics raised money for a new church in two years and his building fund was going on for ten years without collecting one-tenth of the money he needed.

I always meant to get more active in church activities but it was too boring and I never got around to it. Finally Mrs. Berke, the head of the choir, called and begged me to join the choir. They had enough children but not enough older girls. I agreed and went to rehearsal Saturday morning. They gave me my hymnbook and tested my voice. To everyone I was the alto. At night I went over to Berke's house to be fitted for vestments. It was a purple gown with white cape—beautiful. She pinned the hem for me and made a couple of pleats at the side, giving me a Coke to drink while I was standing around in my long robes. Sunday I went early and she had them all sewed and ironed for me.

I got a new suit for Easter—navy and white checks with thirteen possible combinations. The only trouble was each combination looked horrible. An extra navy skirt came with it plus a reversible vest, navy on one side and red the other. I only bought it because I needed something and it fit. I was afraid I wouldn't find anything better, plus Mom kept saying I'd never find a bigger selection for my age group than at Robert Hall's. I thought of looking at Arnold Constable's but they probably would have started at about $60 and this was only $13.95. Mom thought it was a wonderful idea, as though people would really think I had thirteen different suits. You could wear the vest on either side, or leave it off, or wear each skirt with or without the vest, or leave off the jacket and just wear the vest with either skirt, etc. I usually left off the vest and wore the basic suit, checked skirt and jacket together. I wore the navy skirt just as a separate skirt for school. I let the vest go to waste. I wore the suit to church and also to New York when Poll Greenleaf came up and took us to the play.

I went to the Somerset prom with Bob Cerano. I could have gone with John Rourke as he lived in my neighborhood and we knew each other since first grade, but about two weeks before the prom I stupidly let him get mad at me, never thinking of the terrible position it would put me in. I was just carelessly letting the time go by, not thinking about the prom, while everyone else made plans. Joan Guerney was frantically trying to get someone and she snapped up John by asking him over her house the day after I refused to come out for a walk when he called for me. (I was busy doing something in the house, wearing an old pair of pajamas and looking terrible, not even thinking of the prom.) Joan was the last girl (except me) to get a date and I was horrified when I heard he accepted. I was taking him for granted. For five days I was miserable with worry. Then when I had given up hope and couldn't think of what to do with the prom a week away, Bob Cerano caught up with me after school and started a conversation, which I couldn't understand. I didn't even think of the prom until he asked me, even though I was worried. Bob was very intelligent and handsome, just like John Rourke—there was nothing wrong with him. I felt like pushing him off the bike on the ground and covering him with kisses, not knowing why I didn't think of him before. I didn't have a good time at the prom at first but it was better later on. He gave me a gardenia corsage. I could have gotten a new dress (Mom said) but I looked in a few stores and couldn't find anything as good as the one Celia wore to her prom, which fit me perfectly, so I just got it cleaned and it looked terrific. I got white linen heels to go with it. The band wasn't too good. They kept trying to play Dixieland jazz as though they were the great jazz soloists but they couldn't even keep together. After the prom we got together with John Rourke and Joan, plus Lois and her boyfriend Eddie, walking to the highway for pizza at Carl's. Lois had four-inch heels and was going crazy in them. We had a good time although my heels were killing me too toward the end, walking all over. We kidded around a lot and sang at the top of our lungs on the dark streets. I got in about 3:00 A.M.

The yearbook staff passed out a questionnaire asking everyone's favorite song. I decided to ask everyone in the family. Dad's was "As Time Goes By." Mom said she didn't know but finally said "Meet Me in St. Louis." John's was probably "Katy the Kangaroo" or one of the many animal songs he was always playing on his phonograph. He was five and just beginning to come out of his dream world. He used to think Dad was Mom's father. When he got mad at her he started crying saying, "Wait till your father comes home." He would only eat a few things—milk, orange juice, peanut butter sandwiches, cereal, and that was it. He hated the way Mom made eggs. Celia's favorite song was "Summertime." Mine was "You Are My Symphony"—instrumental, "Blue Tango."

Granny sent me a Bulova "Miss America" watch for graduation. Mom and Dad gave me a gold cross. I was glad to get it even though I wasn't religious—it was beautiful and nice to have.

Karl Rovere played a trick on Mrs. Clark as a good-bye to Somerset. We got Clark in eighth grade after getting her in fourth, as she decided to switch to older kids. Our class had the worst luck of any in the school and everyone knew it. The Clark bar as we called her kept us after school fifteen minutes every day and made us drill in the school fields during gym and (supposedly) art. Karl found out her address in Little Ferry and sent her a letter, typing it up on his sister's typewriter. He made it look like an official letter, saying, "Dear Mrs. Clark, I have been observing your performance in your homeroom class at Somerset School for the past three weeks, disguised as a student. Your job as a teacher is to educate, not to provide these shameless emotional displays. You have been put on probation, on my recommendation to the State Board in Trenton. Another observer has been placed in your class to judge your hoped-for improvement. Please try to conduct yourself properly at all times as your job is at stake. Best wishes." He signed a false name with a big title in education. If only he could have gotten some official stationery. Everyone in class saw the letter. The funny thing was a new boy (named John Stokes) just came in the class two days before so she was probably afraid, wondering who he was. We knew when she got it as she came in steaming, not saying anything or knowing what to do but finally she broke down after morning exercises saying, "All right, who's the wise guy?" No one told but there was so much hysterical laughing she knew it was a joke. She was mad but she really looked relieved.

The first day of summer vacation I got sick with terrible pains in my side. I had a headache and couldn't even eat anything without throwing up. Mom took it seriously, saying it might be appendicitis. She called Dr. Taylor and he came in a couple of hours while I lay around moaning and crying. He pressed his hand all over my stomach, asking where it hurt. He said it was appendicitis and I had to get it out. He called an ambulance, which came in about an hour. I got carried into the ambulance on a stretcher, and we drove away with the sirens blaring and Mom sitting by me looking serious (she was sober). I began to have the crazy feeling that it wasn't really my appendix, if Mom hadn't thought of it and called the doctor I would have gotten well the next day. After the excitement of the ride was over and I was lying in the children's ward I began to get scared of having an operation. I started crying and begged Mom not to let them operate as I was afraid of being cut open. Taylor wanted to do it and to me he didn't seem like the wise doctor. Mom felt sorry for me and the tears were rolling down her face as I begged her. She said she wouldn't sign the papers unless it was necessary, and with ether I wouldn't feel a thing anyway. The kid across from me had an operation after his appendix burst and almost died from it. Mom said if they didn't burst it was a simple operation which any doctor could do, including Dr. Taylor.

I didn't know what to do so I had to resign myself to whatever they decided. A nurse gave me a needle in the arm and before I knew it I wasn't worried about the operation, as they wheeled me down the hall to the operating room with everyone trying to comfort me. The doctor who gave the ether was a Japanese. He gave me a big smile and that was the last thing I knew. When I woke up there was Dad holding my hand with Mom sitting on a chair by the bottom of the bed. I couldn't believe it was all over, I was so relieved. My side hurt when I moved but it wasn't too bad. Dad said Mom told him I was incredibly brave about the operation. He bought me a box of candy and some comics. It turned out it was about ten at night. Celia was home with the baby. I couldn't believe it was over, I started crying with joy. The next couple of days I rode around in a wheelchair but the doctor said I should practice walking right away. It hurt a little, not too much, and soon I was back on my feet. It turned out Taylor did a perfect job, as I found out when he removed the stitches six weeks later. It was just a straight scar with even stitches and it was smooth, not like Mom's Caesarean. I got get-well-quick cards from Lois, Judy Dorhner, John Rourke, and Aunt Sally.

A couple of days after I was home Bob Cerano came over on his bike and called for me. I came out to the back yard, still walking slow. Bob had a jar of lightning bugs he caught. He was using it as a headlight for his bike. He offered it to me, saying he could make a ring out of one of them but I didn't want him to "operate."

Aunt Sarah and Tess came up to visit for a few days. They were in Philadelphia for the Republican convention and had souvenirs, buttons, noisemaker, and wood elephant. They were brokenhearted that Ike was nominated instead of Taft, their hero. Aunt Sarah said, "I like Ike, but do I respect him?" They never touched a drop so Mom and Dad cut down while they stayed (a week). I felt nervous with them in the house all day. They cleaned up a little and bought some dish towels for the kitchen. Mom just used regular ones. They probably discovered a lot of messes Mom hid in corners in the kitchen and basement. They got my room and I slept in the sun parlor. (I was near the TV and they went to bed early so it was just as well.) Mom told Celia that Dad used to hate Aunt Tess, who brought him up in her house when Granny was off at nursing school. She wouldn't let him play outside after school, saying he had to do his homework first. He begged to play while it was still light out and promised to do his homework at night. Even though he was an A student she refused. He told Mom he used to cry and write Granny begging her to come get him but she just said to mind Aunt Tess. Now he liked her, always calling her the "salt of the earth." He toed the line when the aunts were around, being glad to have them in the house, but it was a strain on Mom. She drank but didn't really get drunk or start a fight. The aunts didn't notice.

On the weekend they all decided to go to Bear Mountain so we all piled into the car. We went to a new part with a lake and rowboats, plus restaurant and picnic grounds. We had lunch in the "lodge," then Mom and Dad suggested that Celia and I take the aunts for a walk (wanting to stay behind themselves and rest). We reluctantly agreed. Aunt Sarah wanted to go to the lake and look at the rowboats. She leaned on me and Aunt Tess on Celia as they were quite old (68 and 70) even though they liked to run around and see everything. They weren't ashamed to lean. All the races were at the park that day. We passed about a hundred Negro kids on a class trip, then some Puerto Ricans playing ball, talking Spanish a mile a minute. Aunt Sarah's eyes practically fell out as she was only used to "just plain folks" at home but she was still the big expert to me, saying, "You see, everyone can come here, everyone," as though she invented the rules. She could never keep her voice down. A Chinese man walked by us carrying a little boy and I knew she was going to say something. She made a little scene, poking her elbows in my ribs, saying, "Now I expect he's in the laundry business. Don't you bet he's happy to be here where he has his freedom?" He heard and gave us a dirty look. Celia wanted to take them out in a boat, saying we'd both row, but they were too scared and said we'd better find Mom and Dad again. With Aunt Tess holding on to her arm, Celia was trying to make me laugh, humming, "Got a

96

Date with an Angel," which she kept up until we got to the lodge. Mom and Dad were having a good time, drinking coffee and laughing, probably with relief that the aunts were leaving the next day.

The family went to Lake George on Dad's vacation. It was near Celia's college and we dropped her off on the way back. I begged not to go, hoping I could stay home alone and do what I wanted, but they wouldn't agree to that, practically dragging me to the car. I brought a few library books, including *Crime and Punishment*, which was very good. There was an old lady who reminded me a little of Mom, or rather, the way the hero thought about her constantly. I also read *Trailer Trio* and *The House*.

We couldn't go to the place where we rented a cabin the first year because Mom had made a scene there. She wandered off to the main lodge and spent a lot of time in the bar while the rest of us wondered where she was. The owner's wife brought her back, very annoyedly saying we'd better keep her away from the bar. Candlelight Cabins was the new place. It was better, at least for people like us, as it was more secluded and off from crowds. There was a tennis court in a park right by it. Mom wanted Dad to play a little. He couldn't run around or play hard, he wasn't supposed to exert himself as he had a heart condition. The doctor told him he should watch his high blood pressure and keep his weight down. Mom told us to behave ourselves and not make a lot of noise when he came home, although she didn't follow her own advice, plus she made him the same fattening dinner every night—a hamburger with gravy made by adding flour to the grease, all poured over a piece of bread with the hamburger in the middle. Dad hit a few balls back to Mom and even though he didn't run for anything, you could see he was a good player as he made it look easy. Quite a few people gathered around to watch and after he quit a man said to him, "I can see you've played some good tennis." Dad said he'd played quite a lot. He won a few state championships before he got married. The man wanted to buy him a drink, not knowing anything about Dad or us. I guess he could see it in Dad's strokes, even though he was just walking easily around the court. Dad didn't want to talk to him.

I thought I should learn tennis before I was too old to start, but there were no courts around home and no real point to it. Dad had a few silver cups up in the attic and I ran across one Mom won too. We could have shined them up and put them somewhere if we had a den or library.

We did a little fishing but didn't catch much. Dad rented an outboard motor which he showed to the baby, who liked mechanics. We went around the lake in one day and all got sunburned. Mom didn't drink. She got up before everyone else and swam in the lake before anyone was awake. She asked me why didn't I, but I couldn't stand it at first as it was too cold. I forced myself to swim around a little since, as Mom said, what were we there for. Dad said I had the best swimming stroke in the family, I wanted to try the width of the lake but no one wanted to take the boat alongside. Mom dried out, probably wanting to make up for the year before. It seemed like if we could keep her by a cold lake with no liquor all year around she'd be all right, although I didn't like her constant bragging about being up at dawn swimming, and mocking me for taking my time getting into the water. Sometimes I couldn't just run into cold water. We had barbecues at night, cooking hot dogs and barbecued chicken, and toasting marshmallows. The baby had a good time and found a turtle. It was nice and clean out there. Celia and I spread a blanket on the ground at night and looked at the stars—they were big and bright and the sky pitch dark. That was the last summer before she died, although we didn't know it then. We couldn't find any of the constellations although they were probably there as the sky was full of stars.

At Hackensack High I got split up from all my friends and put in a homeroom with a lot of kids from River Edge. I had a terrible desk. A person named "Harry" had it before me and carved his name and initials, H. T., all over it, plus "Harry the Great" in deep letters across the middle. It was a terrible surface to write on and I always had to use a book underneath the paper. I had biology and English in there. When we had tests and nothing was allowed on the desk I had to move the paper all around to keep from making holes in it, plus not press too hard. They usually looked terrible anyway with bumpy letters here and there. A lot of desks were carved but not as much as mine. It must have been boys with pocket knives. I never whittled my name on the desks I got. The kids from River Edge were all in the "fast set" with more money, nice houses, and all going to college. Barbara Eggars, who sat next to me, asked me to come to a pajama party at her house. Sue Wilder, another girl in the class, was going to be there, plus another girl from River Edge I didn't know (Dolores Conti). I got a new pair of blue shorty pajamas and slippers. Dad drove me over to River

Edge Friday night, saying he hoped I had a good time. We had a conversation in the car with him saying he was thinking of starting a farm out West and getting out of the rat race. He asked me how I would like it in the Midwest. I didn't give my opinion as I thought I would take it as it came.

The party was held in Barbara's cellar, which was finished in knotty pine, with an illuminated bar. She had two convertible sofas which we pulled out to sleep on. She had all the latest records. We played the Bill Haley albums and my favorite record, "Two Purple Shadows on the Snow," and practiced dancing to the fast ones. Barbara, Sue, and Dolores were all friends from grammar school in River Edge. Sue was the one who wanted me to come and Barbara did everything she said. Sue had cigarettes and lit one up, offering one to me. I smoked quite a few—I had smoked before at home, using Dad's, just to see what it was like. We all smoked and talked about boys and some of the girls in the homeroom. Dolores brought up the question of what we would do if we fell in love with a Negro. Hackensack High had Negroes and it really woke us up from our dream world. We all agreed we'd marry him if we really loved him, except Barbara. Dolores was going steady but she was the only one. We put on our pajamas and danced some more. Barbara had pretzels and potato chips around which we ate, drinking Cokes. After a while she broke out a bottle of "J & B" from the bar, plus some Ballantine beer, and poured drinks. I had three drinks but didn't feel too different. Barbara had a camera and we took pictures of each other with cigarettes and drinks in our hands. I did imitations of Rosemary Clooney and Joni James to everyone's surprise. Finally about five A.M. Dolores and Barbara dropped off to sleep. Sue and I stayed up, having another drink and talking about school. She said she couldn't stand Barbara's bigoted ways. She said I was like a different person, smoking and drinking. She wanted to give a lot of jam sessions as she called them at her house, and invited me to come. We finally went to sleep and everyone got up late. Barbara's father gave me a ride home in the afternoon. I was in another world and didn't feel like going home. I was still hearing "Two Purple Shadows" ringing in my ears, and felt depressed when I saw the familiar sight of my house. Mom was asleep but Dad was up and gave me a dirty look when I walked in the living room, saying he hoped I had a good time but acting like I was rotten to go. I thought something terrible had happened but nothing had. To avoid an argument with him I cleaned up the kitchen—to make up for my "night on the town."

I would have liked to have pajama parties and raise a little hell but it was impossible. I looked over our living room which was painted light blue, wondering how it would look with floral wallpaper or a leaf design, which Barbara had in her living room. I took a walk to the hardware store to look at patterns but didn't see anything good. When I got back I avoided going up to my room, dreading the gloom, so I started scrubbing the floor in the kitchen, also thinking it would keep Dad from starting trouble with me. He came in while I was singing "Two Purple Shadows" smiling as though we were great friends, asking what I was singing. I said I didn't know and went down to the cellar, hitting a ping-pong ball up in the air until he left the kitchen. Then I finished the floor and had nothing to do. I was hoping Sue would call and ask me over to do homework together, as I hated the solitude of studying, but she was probably doing something with another crowd. She never studied and had a lot of trouble with marks. She thought I was the great student for always doing my homework, not realizing I just did it to keep out of trouble. She said her mother was quite an intellectual, reading the various great writers—Nietzsche, Freud, Omar Khayyam—just for enjoyment. Too bad Sue didn't inherit the interest in reading from her mother, as her habit of never opening a book got her into a lot of trouble at school. I went up to my room and did the algebra, which took about an hour. Dad was still in the living room watching TV. I decided to get the Latin over with too, translating three pages from Caesar's Gallic Wars, which we were just starting. I felt terrific about finishing everything on Saturday night, and at ten Dad went up to sleep. I went downstairs and watched The Late Show (*Harriet Craig*). I made a bacon, lettuce and tomato sandwich and took a couple of his cigarettes, smoking them while I watched the movie. After a while Mom came down to get some milk and watched the end with me. She asked how the party was. I said fine, not mentioning the drinking and smoking. I told her about Barbara's cellar and said we didn't get much sleep, playing records and dancing.

I wrote a letter to Celia telling her how I was getting along in Hackensack High. I had one of her old teachers for biology—Mr. Schultz. Mom wanted to see the letter but I refused as I didn't want to open the envelope. She thought it was about her, I denied it but she didn't believe me, calling me a liar. She suddenly twisted my arm behind my back. I gave up and handed it over. I could have gotten away but I didn't expect her to do it so I just sat there while she got me. She read the letter, probably feeling stupid as there was nothing in it about her. She once found some of Dad's letters to Granny (and Granny's to him) about her, so she probably thought everyone was writing letters criticizing her. She apologized but the next minute she started another fight, saying I never tried to cheer her up or help her and I didn't care about her feelings. All I cared about was high school and my own life and my guttersnipe friends. I said I was always giving advice to help her, "stop drinking," but she never followed it. She said with me going around looking like I had a grudge against her she couldn't stay sober. She said why was I so moody, why didn't I give parties and invite my friends. How could I with that house and her asleep on the floor. I yelled at her to leave me alone. I was upset as I had a lot of homework including a map for Miss Watson due the next day and I was thinking of asking Mom to help me with it. She could be a good artist when she wanted to bother, but naturally it was impossible with her acting like that. I didn't even know where my colored pencils were. Watson assigned it three weeks ago but I just ignored it. Mom called me a worry wart. She always thought my homework was just an excuse. Fortunately she left me alone when I went upstairs, saying she had a much better companion (meaning a drink). I found most of the pencils in my desk and some others in the baby's room. He was always into everything. The map turned out terrible with quite a few smudges and some of the countries looking the wrong shape—it was the Roman Empire. I started crying from frustration but then I thought at least it's done and you won't get into trouble, just forget about it. Sue called about six asking if I wanted to do the algebra over her house and have supper with her. She and her father came by and picked me up. Her mother was sick so her father just got a pizza. I ate with her, her father and brother. He was going to college at Rutgers. She showed me her map, which turned out beautiful as she was a whiz at drawing. I told her about mine and she gave me an artist's soap eraser for the smudges—it made it look quite a lot better. She had a lot of various artist's supplies as she liked to draw. I did the algebra, she did the English, then we traded, saving a lot of time. We watched TV and talked about different kids in our homeroom. Her father drove me home about eleven. Mom and Dad were already asleep.

Monday I had to go the library after school to get books for my biology report. We were on mammals and I got the kangaroo. They didn't have any good books so I just used the encyclopedia and wrote the report there. I learned quite a few new things—for instance, the baby is only about an inch high at birth, surprisingly small considering the size of the mature kangaroo. I thought it was a misprint at first. The big ones can travel about 25 m.p.h. by jumping. After birth the young goes immediately into the mother's pouch and doesn't come out for months. It's a completely different kind of birth from the other mammals. The mother usually has one at a time. I asked the librarian if they had some pictures I could take out and she tried to find some but no luck. I finished around five. Connie Barrone was there doing biology too and we took the 44 home. She had some albums out from the record library—"Rhapsody in Blue," "Slaughter on Tenth Avenue," and some others. She said she loved to drown herself in semi-classical while she did her homework. She said my bangs looked adorable. I didn't bother to write the bio report over as it was oral. Too bad I didn't have a few pictures, but it went fine anyway. It only took about five minutes. I volunteered so I wouldn't get nervous waiting around for Schultz to call on me. I brought up the idea that marsupials were drastically different from other mammals and not only in looks but in the reproduction process. I said the pouch was like a compromise to make up for the short gestation period, if any other mammal that size bore young one inch high it would never live. Schultz thought the report was great but he said I made the common mistake of all his female students by calling the offspring "babies." He said I was a junior scientist so I should say offspring or young. That was his only criticism.

I didn't have much homework, blessed relief. Mom was in a terrible mood. She found my entry to the Rinso contest in my room and made fun of me for entering, saying I lived in another world. She said I had no sense of humor and depressed the hell out of her. It was the old story of how her drinking was my fault. Sometimes when Mom criticized me I thought about being different—always smiling and polite, treating Mom and Dad with respect no matter how drunk they were, and acting like the loving daughter—but I was never in the right mood when I got in a conversation with her.

We got out of school after fourth period as "Ike" was speaking down by the courthouse. The place was jammed with people and we had to stand way in the back. I couldn't hear his speech as the microphones weren't working too well out our way. He looked very handsome for his age and seemed quite serious. Lois and I went window shopping on Main Street after that since we didn't have to report back to school. When I got home I got quite a shock—there was Mom in the living room with an Avon representative. The lady probably thought she had hit the jackpot as Mom was ordering one of practically everything she had. She could probably tell Mom was drinking but didn't care, thinking a sale is a sale. I was going to just creep up to my room but I got scared thinking about the money Mom was spending. I asked Mom to come out to the kitchen, saying I had something important to discuss with her about school. I begged her to cancel the sale, saying we didn't have the money to throw around. I asked how much she had ordered and she didn't even know. I said we had to keep it down to two or three dollars, and she said, "Well, of course, darling." She was just drinking a little and was in quite a friendly mood—that's why she had no sales resistance. We went back in the living room and Mom told the lady she was trimming the list. All she kept on was soap and bubble bath, which she said was a present for me. She was so cooperative I could hardly believe my ears. After the lady left, Mom asked me how school was, just as if nothing happened. Then she gave me a five-dollar bill, saying it was the money I saved by coming in when I did. She suddenly started talking about her childhood, saying she was always miserable when she was young as she could never live up to her mother's ideals. She said she wished she could see her mother just one more time, as it would help her to a better person. She started crying, calling her mother's name saying, "Mother, Mother, help me, help me get out of this."

I wanted to go to the movies Sunday but Mom and Dad said I could only go if I took Johnnie. He was happy to go as it made him feel grown up and I didn't mind too much. We saw *The Bad and the Beautiful* and *Desperate Search* at the Oritani. We had to change seats a few times as Johnnie couldn't see if anyone sat in front of him. It wasn't so crowded Sundays so we could always find a seat with no one in front of it. Johnnie couldn't follow the plots and kept constantly asking me questions. I could hardly hear the movie. Every time a new person came into the story he had to ask, "Is he good?" After about an hour of trying to explain everything to him I was getting frustrated so I just started saying yes or no as the different characters came on. He quieted down and watched the movie, although whenever a new person came in he asked again. Afterwards I took him for ice cream and discovered that he thought Celia was my mother. I explained the family to him, then I asked him questions to see if he understood. He did.

I saw Mom ironing a lot of curled up papers on the ironing board. They were a play Dad wrote in college, which she said she liked to read when she felt low or bored. He wrote it for English, which was the only subject he didn't get an A in. Dad told his professor he worked hard on his themes and couldn't understand why he didn't get an A, as he did in math, history, and his other various subjects. The professor suggested that Dad write a play, promising to give him an A if he did. I read the play, which Dad wrote in longhand. It was about a man named John Livingston who grew up in America but had relatives in England. He was poor although his English relatives were aristocrats. John was summoned to England because his uncle, Lord Livingston, was deathly ill. Lord Livingston was the brother of John's father, who died in America when John was a boy. The family disowned him because he married a commoner (John's mother). John learned he would inherit the Livingston estate if he agreed to live permanently in England. He met a distant cousin, Lydia Morrison, and they fell in love (supposedly). John wanted to renounce the title, asking Lydia to marry him and come to America, but she said it was his family duty to take the title of Lord Livingston. She agreed to marry him when he became a lord, and he agreed. In Act 2, John returned to America, as there was nothing for him to do in England as long as Lord Livingston was still alive. He was determined to use the time to build up the farm he and his mother lived on, which was run down because of drought and lack of money to buy modern machinery. He worked from dawn to dusk to get the farm back on its feet and succeeded. He made enough on his wheat crop to buy farm machinery. He became sick from overwork. His neighbor Ann Middleton, who was the teacher in the local school, came to take care of him because his mother was too weak. Ann was a devoted nurse and very concerned about his health. He recovered and told her about his plans for the farm. He loved Ann but he had promised to marry Lydia Morrison. At the end of Act 2 he received the news of Lord Livingston's death. Act 3 took place in England. Lord Livingston's lawyers demanded that John promise never to return to America. He had to take up English citizenship, and his mother, a commoner, could never set foot on the Livingston estate. John refused the conditions, asking Lydia to return to America with him as his wife. She refused to marry him when she discovered he wasn't going to inherit the estate. She only wanted to be Lady Lydia. John had thought she loved him but was relieved to find out she didn't, as he was free to marry Ann. He renounced his claim to the title and estate. At the end of the play he left the drawing room of the Livingston estate, where everyone was gathered around expecting him to change his mind. Lydia's brother asked him where he was going and he said, "to America!"

Mom started drinking vodka all day instead of wine. She slept more and didn't start arguments with me or anyone. It was peaceful around the house but it was funny to see her so weak and quiet. She was always asleep when I got home and wouldn't wake up before Dad came home. I just let her sleep, thinking it was the best thing. It was like that about a week, then she slept through a whole day, all night, and the next morning she was still asleep. I was worried about her sleeping so long. I didn't even know how long it was. I told Dad we should call the doctor and I'd stay home from school. He agreed. Dr. Taylor came about noon. Mom was still sleeping. Taylor woke her up, shaking her, putting an ice bag on her face, and giving her a shot of something. He said it was going to take time for the alcohol to get out of her system. He said she wasn't eating, showing me how thin her arm was. He prescribed some vitamins for her, telling me if I was the nurse she should have soup, crackers, fresh tomatoes, milk, anything she wanted but no liquor. He told Mom she had a strong constitution or she could never bounce back the way she did but no one could drink so much without ruining her health. Mom said she knew, and maybe she learned her lesson. She was just like a rag doll. He said she should have another baby, saying that would get her on her toes again and give her something to do (stupid). He meant well but didn't understand anything about it.

I stayed home taking care of Mom, bringing her soup, etc. She had an upset stomach and a splitting headache. She was completely sober but felt miserable. She said the idea of a drink made her want to die. She talked in such a weak little voice I almost felt like laughing as it didn't seem like Mom. I wanted to stay out the next day but I had a biology exam. I went to school in the morning but pretended I was still sick. After the exam I got an excuse from the nurse and went home again, bringing all my books so I could stay out a few days and not fall behind. They piled on the homework in high school. Mom got better gradually, saying she could feel the poison draining out of her system. She stayed in my bed. She was so weak she looked just like a baby with her head on the pillow. My room was nice (painted peach by me). I smoothed the bedspread down on my half of the bed and did my homework there. I had some nice days, just heating up soup whenever Mom or I was hungry, or getting crackers and ginger ale which settled her stomach. She said she was beginning to feel human again, and she appreciated me taking care of her as she thought I didn't love her any more. She was back on her feet in a few days but unfortunately it didn't last long as she went back to drinking in spite of all her promises. I thought if she stopped early she'd snap right back so I accused her of drinking (she denied it). I said I was going to follow her everywhere and watch her every minute. She said go ahead, as though she had nothing to lose. After a while she wanted to go in the kitchen alone but I followed her in. She acted annoyed that I didn't trust her, pretending she only wanted something to eat. I went into the bathroom with her, really pushing her around, and found a bottle of vodka in the hamper. She hid liquor there as she could always get away from me saying she was going to the bathroom, and take a drink thinking I'd never know the difference. I continued my plan of keeping an eye on Mom after Dad came home, telling him the reason why so he wouldn't interfere or offer her a drink himself. He sighed as though it was a stupid idea but I could if I wanted to. Mom was getting belligerent and insulting me, saying I was a know-it-all and she didn't know what she did to deserve a dumb person like me for a daughter, but she was just a little annoyed, not really mad. Sometimes she liked to laugh and let me push her around. I made her walk around the block three times, practically dragging her over the snow. All the time she was swearing "goddam you to hell" saying I was going to make her break her neck on the ice. I told her it was to exhaust her so she could fall asleep without a drink. She called me a self-righteous bore but she kept laughing in spite of herself and I did too, as we went sliding over the ice. She fell asleep that night without a drink (I think) but unfortunately the next day she started drinking again. The idea of watching her all the time seemed foolproof but it was impossible because of school, so it only put off the time till she had a drink. Even if I could stay out of school it would get on my nerves after a while to spend every minute playing nursemaid to her and having to look all over the house for hidden bottles, etc. I wasted a lot of time that way and it never did any good in the long run. From being completely recovered she went on another binge, and started pass-

111

ing out again in the day. I found her under the dining-room table after school. The television was on and I couldn't figure out where she was until I heard her snoring and mumbling something and found her lying on the floor. I dragged her up on the couch but didn't bother trying to wake her up. She kept sleeping and I just watched TV.

Joanne Briggs discovered a terrific way to keep socks from sliding—put rubber bands around your ankles and fold the cuff over. My socks were always sliding down, driving me crazy in the halls as I had to stop walking to pull them up with my arms full of books. They would always get too loose. Mom said don't wear loafers but they were the only kind of shoe I liked, the same with Joanne. She gave me some of her rubber bands. I could only find two at home which came around the celery and they were too tight, stopping the circulation. Joanne suggested going to the movies Saturday. We went early and went shopping on Main Street before the show started at 12:00. She bought a couple of bras and I got a garter belt. The movies were *Mighty Joe Young* and *Mildred Pierce*. *Mighty Joe Young* was about a huge gorilla who was brought to America as a circus attraction. A girl had taken care of him from when he was just a few days old, never dreaming he would grow so big. She was the only one in the world he would obey and they did a nightclub act, him holding up a big platform while she sat on it with a piano playing "Beautiful Dreamer," his favorite song. Everyone used to taunt him in his cage and even during performances and finally he went wild, tearing up the city. They only wanted to make money out of him. It ended up with a fire in a big building. A little kid was trapped on the top floor, crying in the window. The girl told Joe to rescue her and he did, climbing up a burning tree with fire falling all around them. The little girl was so afraid of the fire she wasn't even afraid of Mighty Joe Young. Finally he was allowed to go back home. *Mildred Pierce* I had already seen a few years ago. It was the story of a mother who sacrificed everything for her daughter Veda. Mildred Pierce was divorced (partly her fault) when the daughter was only a baby and went to work as a waitress. In a few years she started a restaurant which did very well, then she opened a chain. She gave Veda everything, dancing lessons, music lessons, the finest clothes. She bought a big house and got a colored maid as the housekeeper since she was away most of the time at the restaurants. Veda never knew what Mildred did for a living. One day she discovered her uniform in the closet and thought it was for the maid. Mildred admitted it was hers, saying she worked in a restaurant. Veda couldn't believe it and went wild, saying she was humiliated and never wanted her mother to touch her or come near her again as she smelled like grease. She kept shouting, "Grease, grease, grease!" Mildred just kept giving her more and more—when she was about seventeen she had a fur coat. Finally Veda murdered a man she had been going out with, trying to blame it on Mildred. Mildred was willing to take the "rap" but finally the truth came out. Veda didn't even appreciate Mildred trying to protect her and looked down on her as much as ever as they took her away.

After the show we went to the Oritani Sweet Shop for sundaes. Joanne said she liked movies about human emotion. She liked both but *Mildred Pierce* best. We had a lot of the same opinions. She used to go with Beverly Rainer but she said Bev always wanted to see the comedies and westerns. Joanne and I went quite a few Saturdays after that. She was from Hackensack. We had a few classes together and always walked to English in the halls (with no sock trouble). She said she used to lie in bed in the morning dreading getting up and putting on her socks but now it was such a relief. It was the same to me. She persuaded me to join the school chorus. Once we were talking before the bell in English and all of a sudden I thought I heard a buzzer ring in my head. All the voices seemed to be coming from far away and sweat started pouring down my face. I was afraid but I didn't know what of. Joanne just kept talking, with her face looking bigger and then smaller and her voice going all over the place. I thought I was going to pass out any minute. I gave myself a slap in the face which stopped it. She didn't know what I was doing, thinking I must be crazy. I told her I felt like I was going to faint for a minute. She said all the homework was probably making me flip. When I got home from *Mildred Pierce* Dad insulted me, saying all I ever thought about was my own fun. He said I had a lot of nerve running around with no responsibility to the family. He was drinking naturally, and wanted to force me into cleaning the kitchen. I told him to go to hell and not to bother me when he was drunk. He threw a glass of milk in my face, really drenching me. I almost told Mom, thinking she'd get even for me. I had to wash my hair, change clothes, everything. He was Caspar Milktoast with Mom but he didn't let me get away with anything.

Miss Bristol called me after geometry, saying I wasn't doing such great work and never did the extra-credit homework problems. She always remembered one time when I was the only one to get a problem right, thinking I could be the great mathematician if I just tried, although when I had to explain it on the board I forgot how. It was the old story of someone expecting you to do your best all the time, thinking if you did it once you could do it every time. I told her I had all my other subjects to worry about, not just geometry.

We had a sex education film eighth period instead of gym. Boys and girls saw the same film but in different periods. The film showed pictures of the organs and discussed hygiene and the responsibilities of marriage. It got quite a few laughs in different places. After school I went to the library to get vocational-guidance material to get ready for my appointment with Mr. Graham (guidance counselor). I took out *Right Job for Judith*—the story of a girl who became a secretary. I ran into Joe Vaccara sitting alone at the bus stop. He said he had to stay in at Cory's for detention. Joe was the typical Italian, dark hair, dark eyes, always talking and laughing in a crowd but sad when he was alone with his thoughts. When I got home Mom started a fight, saying she didn't think I could really be her daughter. She was in one of her moods so I didn't even ask what I did.

I got a baby-sitting job over at the Bundys' Friday night. After that I had a steady job for Fridays as they belonged to a club. Lynn was five and always asleep when I got there. She never woke up, always sleeping with a big doll. Stevie was at the difficult age of eight. He was allowed to watch TV with me until 8:30. Then after that if he woke up I had to bring him milk. I was also supposed to listen to his prayers (Catholic) although I couldn't tell if they were right or wrong. Once he woke up saying there was a bear in his room and it turned out to be his bathrobe hanging on the door. It did look like a bear, surprisingly. Mrs. Bundy left cake and milk for me. I sat around in their armchairs wondering what it was like to live in that kind of house. She was the perfect housekeeper, with every room like *House Beautiful.* The second time I was sitting over there the TV was broken and I made the mistake of listening to the radio. "Inner Sanctum" was on, starting with the creaking door and that advertisement. I felt two ways about listening but I wanted to hear the beginning of the story. It was about a man alone in an empty house (supposedly). He heard a woman's footsteps in the cellar, coming slowly up the stairs to him. When he asked who was there no one answered. He didn't know if it was his imagination or someone coming to strangle him. I was going to turn it off and start my homework but I kept thinking just one minute more. I heard a creak in the Bundys' kitchen and began to get scared. It all ended up with me thinking there was someone in the house. I was afraid to turn around and look in the dining room, where I thought he was standing looking at me. I was sitting frozen to the spot trying to get up my nerve. I heard a creak like a footstep in the dining room, then nothing as the man started screaming. I turned off the radio, trying to pull myself together. The house was full of little noises in every direction. I felt like waking up Stevie but I would have felt ridiculous if he told his parents. Finally I went in the dining room and kitchen, putting the latch on the door down to the cellar. Nothing happened but it was nerve-racking to go out there, turning corners all the way. It was just the floorboards creaking. I never listened to that program again except once with Celia, the same for "The Lonesome Traveler," and I would never use that Bromo Seltzer. Another time I was at the Bundys' on Tuesday and "Lights Out" came on. It was the same man from "Inner Sanctum" with a bald head talking in that voice about a spine-tingling tale, supposedly true. I changed the channel even though TV wasn't as bad as the radio where you didn't know where to look. I made about $2.50 or $3.00 each time at the Bundys'. The first time I bought a lipstick, "Strike Me Pink." After that I bought a couple of bras, pants in different pastel shades, plus another lipstick, "Cinderella's Pumpkin," all little things. Then I started saving for big things.

Mrs. Bundy really inspired me with her housekeeping. Saturday I cleaned out my drawers and threw out a lot of old junk. The baby came in and fished out my old Kix Atomic Bomb Ring that I sent off for about five years ago. He wanted to wear it but it was too big for his finger. I told him to take it to Dad, who was downstairs watching the ball game. Dad fixed it by putting tape around the inside so it fit him. I remembered about the secret compartment and went down to show him, but he had just discovered it and was really happy although I don't know who he was going to send messages to as he couldn't even write. After I finished my room I ran the washing machine and did my three blouses and all lingerie. I loved to use the washing machine as it was just press a button and come back later. I burned a hole in my pink nylon slip (my best). I was furious and accused Mom of never teaching me to do anything. I didn't know how hot the iron should be for different fabrics. I didn't even know how to iron. I just tried to iron as I went along, wishing it would be over and turn out all right. The slip didn't even need ironing. After the fight I ironed all my blouses and skirts, feeling terrific as I had my wardrobe ready for Monday through Friday.

I always meant to get organized over the weekends but I hardly ever did. I always had homework and projects to do, plus dirty laundry and no-good clothes.

Joanne and I went to the movies Sunday. There was a western, *Tulsa*, about the discovery of oil in Tulsa, and a foreign movie, *Bitter Rice*. *Bitter Rice* was the story of girls working in the rice fields in Italy. They had to go from place to place in gangs to plant and harvest rice. It was a despressing movie, with everyone sitting around in their slips or undershirts. Some of the girls didn't wear bras. They didn't shave under their arms which was quite a shock and got a lot of laughs. One of the bosses was trying to force himself on one of the girls. She wanted him to leave her alone but he kept following her, she couldn't get away from him as she needed the work. Finally he chased her into a rice-storage building, she had to keep climbing higher and higher up the stairs as he kept following her. She was screaming but no one heard her. He followed her to the top of the tower, when she saw there was no escape she threw herself off. She felt disgraced and she had nothing to live for anyway. She was just a piece of trash as far as the world was concerned, no one cared about her—they just wanted to use her. When she was found dead, all her friends spilled rice over her body. All they got after a year's work was a bag of rice so it was like gold to them. Soon there was a big pile of rice where she fell. Everyone looked sad but they thought it was just part of life. I felt depressed after the movie, feeling guilty about being in America when it was so miserable in Europe and everyone so poor. Whenever a movie gave me a terrible hopeless feeling it always turned out to be foreign. I practically felt like falling on my knees and thanking God for letting me be born in America, as I was pretty happy, even with my family problems. If I lived in Europe I wouldn't have the strength to get through life. Everyone was miserable and knew it, and there was nothing to do. Joanne said it looked like the Marshall Plan didn't accomplish anything. She did a report on it for Drescher and it was supposed to be a miracle in Europe, but in *Bitter Rice* it looked like the war was just over last week. We went to the Oritani Sweet Shop for sundaes, and then she walked me over to Lobell's. I had to get a new gymsuit as my old one was getting tight all over. She invited me over her house for supper. I called home and Dad said okay. We had a terrific time. Her mother was nice—we had lasagna for supper. It turned out that Joanne's brother Pete was adopted. He was happy about it—he thought it was better to be adopted since his parents chose him, he didn't just get born into the family like most people, with no choice for anyone. (That's what his parents told him.)

I caught a terrible cold, probably from standing in the rain waiting for a bus. I dragged myself through school Monday but then I decided to give up and try to recover at home. I stayed home

119

Tuesday and slept most of the day. Mom stayed downstairs and I didn't see much of her, but she brought me some orange juice. I did some English and read a library book, *Emperor's Lady*. Wednesday I still felt lousy so I stayed out again, but it began to get on my nerves. Mom didn't do anything all day. She got up early, then after Dad left she sat around with the TV on and didn't do anything, not even watch. I came down to talk but she wanted to start a fight, as if it was night and I was Dad. She said she was sick of playing nursemaid to me (she brought me orange juice a couple of times). I accused her of not caring if I was sick, she said I wasn't really sick, and it turned into an argument. Mom didn't mind fighting as there was nothing else to do as far as she was concerned. She said if only Celia was there she'd have someone to talk to. I was disgusted about being home so I went back to school Thursday even though I still had the cold. I brought a lot of Kleenex in my bag, and some cough drops. I felt okay although it was too warm in the classrooms. I got so interested listening to Miss Bristol doing a proof on the board I almost forgot I was in geometry. It gave her a shock when she saw my face. She started laughing saying, "Well, I see we have an eager student with us today."

I was on a basketball team which played after school once a week. I didn't like sports but sometimes I wanted to be the great athlete like Mom or Dad, so I signed up for a team now and then. I liked it when the game was over and I could take a shower and feel good and tired before I went home. I went right to bed if there was no interference from Mom, forgetting all about housework. Then I slept until everyone went to bed (missing the eight o'clock fights as Celia jokingly used to call them) and did my homework downstairs while they were asleep. I completely missed Dad that way. It was quiet and I liked the late hours. I spread out all my books and things on the table in the dining room. I would have liked to play forward but my shots weren't that good so I was a guard. I always meant to practice during the summer but I never got around to it. About an hour a day for a couple of months would have made all the difference. The team I was on won the school championship after a play-off. I wasn't one of the big stars of the game but I did pretty well keeping my forward from scoring. In the second half they put me on the high scorer and I slowed her up pretty well though she was fast and a good shot. She had a St. Christopher's medal on a long chain around her neck and I was always afraid it was going to hit me in the eye when she spun around. She was the team captain and gave it everything she had to keep the others going, but she was tired during the second half. She swore at me a couple of times. Toward the end she started getting away from me but time ran out.

After the game we had a victory party with brownies and punch. We had to get back into our gym suits to get our picture taken for the school paper. My hair was straight from the shower so I got a rubber band from the office and put it in a ponytail, which looked all right. As the winning team we all got gold charms shaped like little basketballs. I showed mine to Mom and she said she didn't know I played basketball (after a whole season). I told her I was a forward, just lying for the hell of it. Miss Milhaus said we looked like a gang of refugees but had terrific team spirit. She said I improved a lot over the season. I didn't really get better or worse. I wasn't an even player in any sport. Sometimes I was too aggressive and got yelled at by the referee or Miss Milhaus for crowding someone, and then the next time I'd let people walk all over me, depending on the strange mood I was in.

That night we had the last chorus rehearsal for the winter festival, practicing until we practically dropped. Mr. Sterno picked on the altos saying we were ruining "Night and Day." Naturally he praised the sopranos for everything.

Barbara kept pestering me to have a "jam session" at my house but I kept putting her off as those River Edge kids would have fainted if they saw my house inside. I hated to get rides home from her parties and other events in the daytime as the house looked terrible and I didn't like to point it out to a lot of people. It was old, weather-beaten and looked dirty. I used to pray we could get it painted, but Dad did paint it on his summer vacation and the white paint just soaked in and it still looked gray. Next to the more modern houses on the block it looked like a broken-down farmhouse or, as Mom called it, "the black hole of Calcutta." I wasted a lot of time wondering how it would look if we got shutters for the windows but nothing would really help as it was the wrong shape, design, and color. Changing everything wrong with it would be the same as building a completely new house. I wanted to get high shrubbery in front. Dad got some bushes from a nursery after he finished painting but they were small (about a foot high) and the man said they took ten years to reach full growth. After all that work it looked about the same. Luckily we had screens for summer which looked nice up, adding a touch of green which made the whole house look better in front. They would have kept out the flies too but Mom refused to close the screen doors, so flies buzzed all over the house in summer.

Mom got a little cake and stayed sober as it was Dad's birthday. He bought a new suit as he only had two for work and one was giving out. Mom said I should act nice to him because he was depressed. I didn't even remember Dad's birthday— I had my own troubles. Tuesday nights were always murder, with homework in all subjects and no study periods that day. I had to hole up in my room and I was getting sick of working. I came down and joined their party (they weren't drunk or arguing but acting very serious). I acted friendly to Dad, saying he looked nice in the suit (brown). When they went to bed at 10:00 I brought my English downstairs, which I still had to do chapter summaries plus questions for. I watched a TV show, "Nightmare in Red." It was a documentary special with newsreels showing the Russians spreading the iron curtain around Europe, marching into the different countries, persecuting the church, abolishing free speech, and setting up puppet dictators. They showed the dates as each country fell down to Russia. There was a map and as the country turned Communist it turned black on the map. At the end of the show practically everything was black. I was so depressed after the program I could hardly concentrate on my Ivanhoe, not knowing what was going to become of the world or democracy. I washed my hair in the kitchen and made hot chocolate (drinking about four cups). Then I read the two chapters while I set my hair. When I finally finished the summaries and questions it was about 2:00. I was exhausted and fell right asleep.

As a member of the winning basketball team I had a chance to join the Girls Sports Council. Meetings were held after school every Friday. They had the tradition of a progressive dinner every year before Xmas holidays. Each member had a course at her house with everyone driving around from house to house until the dinner was over. Miss Milhaus and Miss DePenna brought their cars and some of the seniors had cars too. It started at 7:30 and ended around midnight. I stupidly signed up for the soup course, saying my mother's specialty was vichyssoise. Mom made it a couple of times, saying it was the food of the gods. I should have made an excuse, saying there was illness in the family, but I didn't want to for a change. I thought it would turn out all right somehow and it would be a good step to being popular. Everyone called me "the French chef." I couldn't do any of the work on the house, as I had a lot of homework (as usual) and also had to play volleyball after school to stay in the Sports Council. I told Mom she had to make the vichyssoise and clean the house, it was the only big favor I asked her in years and the first time I ever "entertained" as she would call it, which she was always saying I should do. We needed a soup tureen and about two dozen soup plates. She said she'd fix everything. I was getting nervous about everything, thinking of so many girls from school, plus two teachers, in our living room. The night before, doing homework late, I was looking at the furniture in there and I began to feel hopeless about the room ever looking nice. The

124

slipcovers had holes in the arms, we also had a padded rocking chair with the springs sprung. You couldn't sit on it unless you were used to it. The end table by the couch had bumps all over from Mom's and Dad's hot coffee cups which melted the varnish, then it dried that way. The lampshades were all dirty with strings hanging off them. I cut off the strings. Thank heavens I put up "wheat" wall-paper in there on the Thanksgiving holidays. There was nothing to do about the furniture even though I was crazily expecting Mom to perform a miracle.

All the next day I thought I should tell Miss Milhaus to cancel my course, making up some excuse, but I was too embarrassed and kept thinking Mom would come through somehow since it was so important. After school a nagging voice told me to hurry home and see how things were, but my team was scheduled and if I didn't go I'd feel funny that night since the Sports Council was supposed to be great on attendance. I was getting into my gym suit, carelessly talking to Carol Schneiderman, but all the time wondering how Mom was. Finally I got home about six, I was supposed to get over to Sandy Chumley's for the first course at 7:30 and just about had time to change. Mom was drunk with the living room a complete mess. She had all the furniture in the middle of the room and she was on her hands and knees scrubbing the floor in the corner with a little piece of steel wool. I went wild with fury. I thought it was impossible she would be like this when it was really important. The part she was scrubbing didn't even show. It was under a chair. She made a big white patch with the Brillo on the dark floor. She kept going over the white part, as if everything was almost ready. She didn't even vacuum or dust. She acted like everything was fine, saying, "Oh, hello, darling." I started yelling at her, and almost broke down crying but I didn't even have the time to. I thought I should call Miss Milhaus with any excuse but I was afraid everyone would see through it. Then Dad came home. He knew about the progressive dinner and was panicked when he saw the living room and Mom. He asked me when they were coming and I said about two hours. He said he'd try to fix things up. Luckily Mom had bought fifteen cans of vichyssoise which were out in the kitchen, also a tureen with a matching ladle. She must have started out sober in the morning but then started drinking when she got back from the store.

Dad drove me to Sandy's at 7:30. I was late but they hadn't started eating yet. She had a beautiful house, her father was rich (a dentist), and everyone sat down at a big table in the dining room, under a golden chandelier. It was so different from my house I almost fainted thinking all those people were going to eat at my house. Sandy's mother served the appetizer, staying in the background. Everyone had a great time. A couple of girls said they could hardly wait for the vichyssoise, which they never had. After Sandy's we went to Marie Panelli's for Italian antipasto. She had a poorer house in South Hackensack with linoleum on the floor but still nice. Her mother was the fat happy type. We stayed about a half hour there and then it was to my house. I could hardly think or talk all the way. I just acted like I had to concentrate on the directions of how to get there (wanting to give the wrong ones). When we pulled up at the front door, Dad came out, putting on a big smile to everyone. The house looked all right outside as it was dark with just the porch light on. I ran past him into the living room with dread but it was a wonderful surprise. He had put all the furniture back and vacuumed, and started a fire in the fireplace. It looked beautiful and with all the other lights out it just gave a soft light and you could hardly see the furniture or rug. The dining room looked just as good, with no lights on and just three candles on the table. It looked like a party atmosphere. He had the soup tureen out and all the cups and spoons around it. He told me to sit in the chair with the bad springs. Everyone came in and sat around on the couch and chairs but mostly on the floor by the fire. Then Mom made her grand entrance down the stairs, all cleaned up and quite sober, acting like the guest of honor. She made a big hit with everyone, monopolizing the conversation and saying to me, "Darling, why don't you do the serving honors?" I stood at the end of the table and filled a cup for everyone as they came by, buffet style. Everyone complimented Mom on the vichyssoise and she laughingly told them the brand name. I was boiling in the dining room, listening to her talking, wondering what she was going to say next. She brought up the question of Negroes, saying she noticed there weren't any there, yet she knew they were good athletes. Miss Milhaus explained there were a couple of Negro girls in the Sports Council but they made different excuses for the dinner. Mom said it was a shame they felt that way, and kept on talking about different things. No one could get a word in edgewise. It was amazing how fast Mom could sober up and act superior to everyone. Dad stayed out in the kitchen peeping his head in once in a while to see if he should bring refills. Before I knew it, it was time to go to the next course. I was furious at Mom but really relieved it was over. I was grateful to Dad as he saved my life.

Dad got a promotion! It was a surprise to him—he got called in to a meeting after lunch and his boss told him then. Dad called Mom from the office he was so excited, and she told me when I came in the door after school. She was pretty sober and trying to get things in shape for when he came home. When Dad came home he was overjoyed. He brought some Chanel No. 5 as a present for Mom and said that was just the first installment. Mom was happy and said all his years of hard work were beginning to pay off. She said he should buy a new suit. Mom said a raise went with it but Dad said the big thing in the long run was the promotion. He wanted to get all his debts cleared up. I congratulated Dad, saying I was glad they had the brains to appreciate his work. He said you can always count on that in the long run. He said to get myself something I wanted, giving me $20! He was going to take Johnnie to a store and buy him a model railroad. Mom sang her favorite song, "Meet Me in St. Louis." She looked pretty nice. They didn't drink when I was there as they knew how I was against it, but broke out a bottle to celebrate when I went up to do my homework. Dad was talking about buying a car.

I decided to use Dad's money for cosmetics and went on a shopping spree with Sue Saturday. She said her only beauty treatment was wash her face with Noxzema, then rub in about half a jar every night. She had a nice complexion so I decided to try it and got a big jar of Noxzema. I wanted to find a good shade of lipstick for me. Sometimes I just bought them by the name and didn't really look at the color. Mom got me a new Hazel Bishop which I was trying to use up, but I decided to just throw it out as it was dark red and made me look sick (too pale). I went to Arnold's and sampled different brands with Sue. Some of the names sounded so different but when you put them on it was just red or orange. I decided the shade for me was just plain "peach." Sue got a "Persian Melon." She said the best hand lotion was Pacquins so I took her advice again and got a jar. I also got a blush rose compact and brown mascara. It all came to $3.50. We went over to the Knitwear Shoppe and I got five pairs of white knee socks— that way I could just run the washing machine on the weekend and not worry about it school nights. I also got a navy jumper and a red and white striped blouse at Knitwear. It was quite a lift for my wardrobe. Then we went over to Rainbow and I got a negligee.

Mr. Schultz was sick and we had a substitute, Mr. Burt. Mr. Burt very cynically said war was good because it kept the population from getting out of control, by killing men in their reproductive years. Otherwise, according to him, it would be starvation. He had a big smile on his face but he was serious. Schultz came back in a few days and we went back to his method of biology—describing the animals, learning the phyla, etc.

Sue caught chicken pox and was out for two weeks. I went over her house after school and brought her her books and assignment. She had some scabs on her face but it was clearing up. She was glad to be out of school and really looked happy propped up in bed with the radio, soda and cookies by her bedside, etc. Her mother made me a toasted peanut butter sandwich, which I never had before and it was pretty good. I told Sue all about school. She was worried about social studies because she thought Garrick was going to give her a hard make-up for a test she missed. She thought he didn't like her. She missed two chapters, city government and conservation. I told her about cooking class Thursday. Jeannette Andrea couldn't light her oven and finally it came on with a big explosion when she had her head stuck in. It really gave her a shock and singed her eyelashes. The whole class nearly jumped out of their skin, but we couldn't stop laughing. Miss Hester put her arms around Jeannette and didn't accuse her of incompetence as she usually did if someone made a mistake, but she bawled out the class for laughing. She must have been in a good mood though as she let us eat our cookies for a change. Sue broke up laughing, saying everything happened when she was away. Her mother came up and said to calm down, she was still sick. I stayed late as I didn't have any homework to worry about. Her mother asked me to supper and brought up a tray for both of us. About 8:00 her parents went out. Sue wasn't supposed to get out of bed but we went down to the den in the cellar and watched TV. She was leading the life of Reilly since she got sick. We watched "Mama" and a Charlie Chan movie, plus parts of some other movies. Sue got out some pretzels, potato chips and Coke. She said being sick made her realize how wonderful life could be if there was no school—everything you learned could be compressed into about an hour a day anyway. Her brother came home about midnight and gave me a ride home from River Edge. He said he thought Sue had been well for about a week but didn't want to admit it. I said she was still sick as her face was covered with

130

scabs. He asked wasn't I afraid of catching chicken pox but I explained I had them when I was small.

Sue was a nice kid but she was getting in with some tough kids from Hackensack who liked to play a game called knuckles. The one who lost got hit on the knuckles with a pack of cards. Every player was supposed to hit hard and scrape the edge of the deck over the loser's knuckles, if they went easy they were supposed to get the "knuckles" treatment from everyone else. She came out of one game with her hand all cut and bruised.

Dad got a new car—a '48 Chrysler, blue, which looked completely new as a single businessman had it before. We all went for a ride and had a pretty good time. Johnnie sat on the seat divider in the back. Dad dropped into a Howard Johnson's without anyone asking and got ice cream cones for the whole gang.

I got a letter from Yvonne Reese. She moved to California a year ago as her father wanted to start a career out there. He said no one in the East had a chance. In the letter she said she met a few nice kids in school although in general the girls wore too much makeup, always expecting to be discovered by Hollywood. A lot of them wore stockings to school every day. She said she was much healthier with all the sunshine and finally got to give up acrobatic dancing. As a joke she said that getting away from Radio City Music Hall was the best break she ever had. Her mother always had the ambition for her to be a Rockette someday and forced her into lessons although Yvonne hated them—she had asthma and they always brought on an attack of suffocation. She had a boyfriend (seventeen) with a car. She wore lipstick every day and a little powder. I wrote her back all the news, saying everything was the same "out East."

I gave my book report in English—*The Greene Murder Case*. It was about "the perfect murder," the victim was stabbed with an icicle. Naturally it melted so no one could find the murder weapon. After school I went shopping with Lois. She had just gotten a check from her father and brought a couple of negligees at Rainbow. I got a couple of pairs of white wool socks. I stopped off by the library and returned a lot of books I had out for different reports, including *The Greene Murder Case*. After that I had no books to carry around as I did my homework in study period so I really felt carefree. We got on the wrong bus from Main Street and ended up in Hasbrouck Heights—we thought we were on the 44 but it was the 54. We were scared as it got dark early and we didn't want to get on another bus since the bus drivers didn't like to give directions and we might end up down in Jersey City. It was no use for Lois to call home— her grandmother couldn't understand anything on the phone and would just get panicked. I called Dad from the Hasbrouck Heights bus terminal and he agreed to pick us up. He had just got home from work. I don't know how he found Hasbrouck Heights but there he was in about a half hour. He said even though we were learning all the higher mathematics we still had to keep our feet on the ground about bus numbers. He was just joking around. He was happy—I think because the car was just washed and looked nice and shiny. Lois said he saved our lives.

I told Dad I had a terrible nagging backache. Maybe it was from carrying too many books around Hackensack High all day, or just tiredness. He said my mattress was probably too soft. He took a look at it and said it was shot—he and Mom bought it when they got married and then Celia and I used it when we got their old bed, so it was pretty old. Dad said I needed a new one and it was a good investment as people spend about a third of their lives in bed. We got it about two days later and sure enough my backaches went away.

Rev. Lanford persuaded Mom to try A.A. and Mom got to know quite a few people in it—Helen, Alice, and Jean. They came by the house once in a while to talk about A.A. and how it could help an alcoholic. They drank coffee and told Mom about their own experiences. Alice was Mom's sponsor before she gave up—quite happy and gay. She had a tan and wore a different dress every day which she made herself. Once she crocheted a dress in a week out of thick blue thread. Alice said she threw away her life for years drinking and was a terrible wife and mother. At a party she once poured whiskey into a lady's shoe and drank out of it. She broke her ankle falling off a piano which she was standing on singing at the top of her lungs. Mom asked didn't her life seem dull now, devoting all her time to not drinking. Alice said she was an alcoholic and couldn't touch a drop without becoming a hopeless drunk. She said Mom couldn't stop drinking until she admitted that about herself. Mom repeated her question about life being dull if all you thought about was not drinking. Alice laughingly said it solved the problem of "the meaning of life," as she knew her purpose in life every day was not to break out a bottle. She said she was proud of how she changed her life and had never been so happy as when she stopped drinking (six years ago). Jean was another story. She was the black sheep of the Ridgewood group and Helen and Alice agreed she had no business "helping" Mom as she was always drinking herself. Jean came around quite often anyway—she had a weird interest in Mom. She hated me, thinking she and Mom were better than anyone. She was the worst possible influence for Mom, always hinting I was responsible for her drinking. Helen and Alice acted like they knew I must have been through hell with an alcoholic mother although I never said anything to them, but not Jean. Once when I came home from school I found her sitting in the living room looking like she owned it. It gave me a shock because I thought it was Mom until I saw Jean's horrible face. She wanted Mom to come over to her house (by a lake) to get away from Dad for a few days. Mom was upstairs packing. Jean tried to start a conversation with me, saying she wanted us to play a little game together. She asked me to name all the costumes I wore for Halloween starting with kindergarten up to seventh. I agreed. It was kindergarten, fireman, fifth grade, harem girl, all other years, witch. She smiled like the great psychiatrist, saying it was just as she thought. She said all my life I tired to get a great sense of power by trying to scare the world (by pretending to be a witch) except for one year when I tried to be the sex siren and failed. I denied it. Jean very arrogantly said she knew more about me in five minutes than I'd ever know in a lifetime. She was drinking but naturally thought no one could tell. I went upstairs and begged Mom not to go with her (Mom was sober), which Jean heard and added to her hatred. Mom decided to go for the rest, saying she'd be back in a couple of days and to tell Dad.

When spring came they had tryouts for cheerleading. There were four seniors graduating so four places were open for the next year, as Sharon Bertone (the captain) announced at the victory rally for the last game of the season when we trampled Our Lady of Sorrows about 46 to 0. All the cheerleaders sat up on the stage wearing the blue and gold outfits and Sharon gave a talk saying the cheerleaders' job was to whip up school spirit at the games. She encouraged everyone to try out in the spring and closed the assembly with the "Hack, Hack, Hackensack" cheer, each time getting louder and everyone stamping their feet until it felt like the walls were shaking. Everyone wanted to be one so they started with practice classes for everyone who came out. They did acrobatics to limber up for the final tryouts (when everyone had to go through the cheers in front of judges, including Miss Milhaus). It was harder than it looked, jumping up with those heavy saddle shoes and touching the back of the head with the feet.

I didn't feel like trying out but I kept thinking about it. I didn't even go to the games too often as I couldn't get caught up in the excitement. The night before the practice classes began I had a dream where a voice came to me (God?) saying, "This is your last chance." This was really true as they would select cheerleaders in a month and the next year I'd be too old. I went down to watch the first session, which about a hundred girls came to. Everyone wore their gym suits or shorts and skirts. Sharon and Marie Zeller divided the girls into two groups and led them through some exercises. A lot

135

of girls came to watch and I stood around there. Finally I decided not to try out, thinking for one thing I wouldn't have the strength to go through with it. About half the girls dropped out the first week. Some of them were really black and blue, sore from all the exercises, practically limping in the halls. About twenty-five made it to the tryouts. The four selected were Virginia Dean, Sandra Cerelli, Carole Schneiderman, and Sharon Weber. There was a new Sharon to replace the old one. I felt terrible when it was all over, not because I really wanted to be a cheerleader all my life but I had always thought in the back of my head that I might be one and then I knew I never would be.

I got back my personality inventory. It showed the fields that would fit in best with a person's personality and likes and dislikes. Mine said I should avoid fields that required persuasion (sales work or teaching or politics) or competition. My highest score was to be a musician (too bad I couldn't play an instrument). Next to that it was medical research. Even though I didn't like science too much I began to think about trying it, thinking maybe some day I could find the cure for alcoholism, although probably no one could be that great a genius.

Jean Houghton whisked Mom off to her summer house—we didn't even know what town. Dad just gave up. I called Alice and told her. She was sorry but her son was in the hospital so she didn't have time to look for Mom. Mom was gone five days. The house seemed empty and I was always wondering where she was. She came back on Monday, as I discovered after school, finding her in the living room with Jean. Mom was glad to see me but Jean gave me a dirty look. She pretended to be friendly but couldn't hide her real feelings (hatred), saying, "I suppose you're overjoyed to have your Mommy back," very sarcastically. I asked Mom where the hell the house was—it turned out it was Lake Packanack. Mom and Jean were drinking and eating toasted cheese sandwiches. Mom offered to make one for me and I accepted. I asked her if she was home to stay and she said yes. She was drinking but not drunk as the trip was a break from her old routine and brought her out of her shell. Jean barged into the kitchen with my looseleaf. She found an English test I got 80 on, saying, "Not so hot—I thought your mother said her girls were perfect little students." I was steaming but politely told her to please not go into my private papers. If only Alice could have come she would have been a far better influence on Mom. Jean wasn't Mom's sponsor, wasn't a member in good standing at A.A., and wasn't even sober. She just used A.A. to find people who liked to drink and everyone in A.A. knew it. She was a terrible influence on Mom but it was Mom's own fault— everyone warned her about Jean. Out at the lake they had a lot of time to discuss things, including me and the contest I won for the essay on Dad. Jean pretended to congratulate me, saying very sarcastically she was anxious to read it as she was sure it was brilliant. I wanted to go up to my room with my sandwich but Mom said I should stay down with her and her guest as she hadn't even seen me in a few days. I reluctantly agreed. Mom was drinking wine, not hiding it as Jean was there drinking too. Jean discussed her son who was one of the many people she didn't like. He couldn't go to a regular school as he couldn't even pass first grade, couldn't learn to read, and was always hitting people. Finally they had to send him to a military school. Jean said he was improving but he was still stupid. She didn't even love her own son, though he probably got that way from having Jean for a mother and following her terrible example. Mom said she didn't approve of the strict discipline of military schools, but Jean said, "Wait till you meet my little Georgie." She started talking about Alice, sarcastically calling her "Miss Iowa." Then she asked me about my schoolwork, my hobbies, my interests, my boyfriends, and so forth, pretending to be fascinated by everything I did. I said I had work to do and went upstairs. I couldn't concentrate on my homework so I just lay on the bed flipping through a magazine, listening to them mumbling and laughing downstairs.

Finally Dad came home. He was surprised to see Mom back home with Jean, but he just acted normal, not wanting to cause a scene. I could hear them having a conversation and Dad probably having a drink with them. They got into an argument, with Jean laughing at everything Dad said even though he was trying to be serious. No one said anything about when Jean was going to go home. I was frustrated as I couldn't do anything with all the commotion, so I went down. When I got to the living room there was Jean telling Dad, "Oh, Harry, you're such a colossal bore." I asked Jean when she was going home, which gave her a shock as she didn't know I was there. She acted like the great movie star, looking at me as though I was the little jerk who just barged in, laughingly saying, "Who do you think you are, you arrogant little bitch?" She was always asking for it and never expecting to get it. I told her to never come back to our house again and never bother Mom again, if she did I'd report her to the police. She laughed as though I was so ridiculous. I hit her and pushed her across the room with all my strength as she tried to hit back. She went flying across the room, landing on the sofa and hitting her head on the wall. I told her to never talk like that to me or my father again. She was shocked at me (even though she was supposed to say anything she felt like). I was more than a match for Jean in her drunken condition (she was a stringbean too) and she knew it. She got her coat as if it was her idea to go. She gave me a dirty look, saying good-bye to Mom but nothing to me. Mom and Dad thought I acted terrible but they agreed Jean was asking for it. I was glad to see the last of her. Mom said it did her a lot of good to have a vacation away from the house, but she was glad to be home. Dad was mad about her leaving and didn't want to discuss it. It was a quiet evening at home after that with them watching TV and me upstairs. "I Love Lucy" had a baby boy.

On Easter vacation Sue, Barbara, and I went to Palisades Park. Barbara had discount tickets so on Tuesday we could go on all the rides for 5¢. It was supposed to rain Tuesday but we went anyway. It turned out for the best because it didn't rain after all and it wasn't crowded, with no lines for the rides. They had a new ride called "The Thing"—a big barrel that spun around, then the floor dropped out and you stuck to the wall by centrifugal force. It wasn't too good even though it sounded exciting. I wore my navy slacks with red and white striped polo shirt and loafers. We went on all the rides—the Rocket, Tilt-a-Whirl, Flying Saucers,

Cuddle-Up, Whip, Bug, Twist, Caterpillar, Tornado, and a couple of others. I had to put my hair in a ponytail as I couldn't keep it under control. Sue got sick and we had to sit out a few. We were going to go home early but she felt better after we sat on a bench for a while. She ate some plain popcorn and it settled her stomach. It turned out to be a beautiful day with blue sky and clouds and the sun out. It was windy which made the rides more exciting when you got up high. I loved Palisades Park as there was always something to do, and the sounds of rides and people yelling and screaming always in the air. We went up in the ferris wheel and saw New York, with the skyline, boats on the river, etc. Some boys in another car were trying to scare us when the ferris wheel stopped with us at the top, saying our cable was about to snap. We knew they were only kidding but I was relieved when we got down to the ground again. The boys started following us around, asking us to go on the roller coaster with them. They were seventeen, from Union City. One of them, named Vince, kept saying there was nothing to be scared of and it was the best ride there. They called it "The Cyclone" at Palisades Park. Finally we all agreed. Vince liked to kid around, saying "do you want roses or lilies?" as we got to the top of the first hill on the roller coaster. I was scared as we slowly rolled up to the top but once we started down there was no time to think. I was glad I did it. Vince had a nice personality and wasn't afraid of anything. I told him I was glad he talked me into the roller coaster, which was the one ride I always used to skip. The boys wanted us to watch them shoot at the ducks in the rifle booth and we went along. Vince won a piggy bank which he gave me. Eddie and Bob won little dolls which Sue and Barbara got. It was lucky it was three boys, three girls. It got chilly so they gave us their jackets to wear. They were all in a club called the "Heavenly Devils." We went in the photo booths in the arcade. Vince wanted to get his picture taken with me and I agreed. He gave me one. (He looked serious in the picture.) Sue really came to life again and was having a great time with Eddie. Vince and I exchanged telephone numbers but we never got in touch after that. When we came out of the arcade it was pretty dark, all the lights were coming on which really looked beautiful. You could hear the crazy laughing from the fun house which really made you want to go in. I would have liked to stay all night but we had to get home. The boys persuaded us to go for pizza. They had beer and we had a few sips. We said we were seventeen. I had a great time, it was the best day I ever had. We just caught the eight o'clock bus. I was afraid I was in for it as I told Mom I was just going for the day, but no one said anything when I came in about nine with my bank.

I didn't have anything to do Saturday so I did my Latin for Monday. We were on "The Labors of Hercules," and Watson was piling it on so we could get to the great classics by spring. It took about two hours to do one page of translation. About ten o'clock I got an emergency call from Miss Bedford. She wanted me to substitute as a Sunday School teacher in the kindergarten class as the regular teacher was sick. I agreed. The class was the youngest—4 and 5 year olds. They just colored pictures and all got a sticker of a bird or flower, passed out by me, to paste on a picture of Jesus out in nature. It was the noisiest table in the room, as they had arguments about the crayons and supplies. Each one had a different personality. When the movie came on they didn't understand it although the older kids were quiet and paid attention. The movie was quite inspiring, showing the miracle of Lazarus.

Monday I was late for lineup in gym and had to see Miss Milhaus after school. My locker got stuck and I had to do the combination about ten times before it opened. She gave me a dirty look when I came in her office, keeping me waiting about 20 minutes while she went out to the gym, yelling around as they put up the nets for the volleyball teams. As a member of the Sports Council I was supposed to feel terrible about being late. Finally she came back and asked what happened. I said my lock must be rusty inside as it was always jamming. She said when she blew the whistle she wanted the girls in their squads, at attention, with pressed gymsuits and clean sneakers, and no excuses. To her gym was the most important class in school—she was the tomboy who never grew up. I got a demerit but she said it would be wiped out if there were no more offenses that marking period. It was a relief to get out of there but I was afraid I'd be late again the next day as my lock wouldn't budge half the time. I felt like going home but I got my nerve to go back and ask her if she had some oil I could put in the lock. She had a little can of 3-in-1 and it worked perfectly. I practiced opening it a few times before I went home. The lock didn't give me any more trouble but I was always nervous in gym after that as I was on Milhaus' black list and I couldn't stand her eyes staring at me.

Mom called me a yankee. It really hurt my feelings as to her it was the greatest insult. She never said it before. We didn't get into a long fight, I went up to my room and she stayed in the living room. I didn't have any homework as I did it all in study period. I read a library book, *White Tower*.

Mom and Dad got into a fight, it was one of the worst yet. It just dragged on. Neither one of them got tired, so each time I thought it was going to die down it just started up again and got worse. It was Saturday night. The fight was about money and how each one hated the other for ruining their lives. They wouldn't stop even though I went downstairs twice to try to break it up, complaining about the noise and saying I couldn't sleep. I really envied the baby being able to sleep through it all. Finally I was furious and going crazy with all the yelling, and trying to think of what to do I got the idea of going to see Celia at school. I took $15 from Mom's purse and just threw a couple of things into a canvas beach bag. I didn't leave a note or anything. They didn't notice me walking out even though I went right past them in the living room, although they both kept quiet a couple of minutes. They probably thought I was just going into the kitchen and forgot I didn't come back. I got on a bus at the corner of Chestnut going to the Port Authority, it took about an hour to get to New York. I knew all I had to do to get to the college was get on a bus at the Greyhound Station on 34th Street, and ride about six hours. I walked over from the Port Authority, as it's on 41st Street. First I walked the wrong way up to 44th (I couldn't get used to New York), but then I went the right way and got to 34th Street without any trouble as all the streets were numbered. I got a round-trip ticket for $8.80. Luckily I only had to wait an hour for the next bus to leave. It was a strange (safe) feeling traveling in the dark with no one knowing where I was, although I was worried about what Celia would say when she saw me.

The bus got to the college early in the morning. I was awake and saw the sun come up. I had to get a cab out to the school ($1.25). I didn't know where Celia's room was so I went to the main building where lights were on. There was a night watchman there but he said nothing was going to be open until 7:45. I waited around till then, and then called Celia from the phone there. She was surprised to hear from me. At first she was afraid I was calling from home and something had happened. She came over to the switchboard and said I could have breakfast with her in the student dining room. I had to buy a guest ticket (35¢). She said fortunately none of her friends got up early for breakfast on Sunday so we could talk freely. Only one girl in the whole college went to church and she was at a table eating by herself. I told Celia Mom and Dad were fighting and driving me crazy, and how Mom was always criticizing me and calling me names after school. Celia said I should remember I could leave home in a few more years and all I had to do till then was hang on. She said she had a campus job (not to tell Dad) and she could pay for my meal tickets if I wanted to stay a few days. I could sleep in her room as there was an extra mattress around to put on the floor. She asked a lot of questions about Johnnie, saying he was old enough to know what was going on and I should talk to him, explain things to him, and tell him what to do. She asked me why I always called him the baby when he was already in school. She called home around noon so they wouldn't call the police when they found me gone. She said she had a lot of work, two papers to hand in at the end of the week, but I could stay in her room and read or go to the movies with her or any of her friends if they were going. I stayed even though I was worried about missing school. (I was out a whole week.) Seeing Celia study made me think about all the work I'd have to make up when we got back. I had brought my *Word Wealth* with me and I learned a couple of chapters ahead while Celia was pounding away on the typewriter but I knew it wouldn't help much compared to the biology, history, and geometry.

Celia's best friend Anna came over a lot and talked about their teachers, etc. I didn't mention the problems at home—just said I was coming for a visit even though my parents didn't think I should since it wasn't a vacation. Anna was a happy girl, always laughing with a lot of cynical remarks about people, but sometimes acted down in the dumps and disgusted with school and life. Jeanne, a girl who lived across the hall from Celia, came over a couple of times when Anna was there. The three of them got into a conversation. They all smoked and so did Celia. They talked about philosophy and the Renaissance (a course they were all taking). Celia said wasn't it funny that in the Renaissance everyone thought the Greeks were greater and tried to imitate them and today we think the Renaissance art is just as great. Jeanne said no one thought that and if Celia understood Greek art she wouldn't either. They had a lot of different opinions. Anna said people always think some other life is greater than their own times and Celia and Jeanne agreed, although Jeanne said we didn't have respect today for anything in the past.

They started talking about sex, which Jeanne said was overrated. Celia and Anna said it wasn't. Anna brought up the subject of orgasms, saying without that she'd have no reason to go on living. Celia and Jeanne didn't say anything. Celia brought up the idea of how to make love a real feeling, not just an idea. I wanted to ask them what they really knew but they were talking like the big experts so I didn't say anything. Celia brought up the time I told Mom and Dad a dream I had, with telephone poles and a big cactus chasing me across the desert (all symbols for sex). Anna said her ambition was to be an actress and eventually get into the movies as that was the only thing anyone respected in our society.

One night we went to a movie on campus (free). It was an old movie called *Ninotchka*—about a Communist from Russia who came to Paris on government business and met an American there. She was an officer in the Russian army and always wore a uniform. She fell in love with the American but with her Russian training she thought it was wrong to try to have a happy life, or even smile, when the world needed to be reformed. He finally made her see the carefree side of life and all the things there were to do in Paris. At the end she escaped from Russia and they got married.

Another night Jeanne, Anna, Celia and I went to a drive-in in Jeanne's car. It was *I Was a Teen-Age Werewolf*. They liked the movie, treating it like a joke. After the movie we drove out to a place called "The Pine Cabin" for westerns on toast. Jeanne said they never got enough to eat at school and were always starving about ten every night. They couldn't go to bed early as they had to study late with all the work they got. It turned out Jeanne came from a rich family and lived on a big estate. They discussed Hobbes, who they were writing papers about. Hobbes had the philosophy that men need a strong ruler to keep peace, or they'll constantly fight over land, food, power, and different things. Anna brought up the question of whether man was naturally good or evil. Jeanne said man was born good, the evil in a person came from an unhappy childhood. Celia said man is naturally evil, the good came from childhood, learning the laws of civilization, etc. Anna agreed. It was the kind of argument no one could win, as no one really knew.

Thursday I called Mom in a fury and told her to call Peter Deller for my homework early at night when she was sober and to get my biology book home—it was the only one still in my locker. I said I'd come home in time for school Monday. She was surprised at how I was acting and agreed right away. I caught the bus home Saturday morning so I'd have Sunday to catch up on some of the work. Anna drove me to the bus station as Celia had classes and we stopped off for a Coke along the way. She said Celia was her best friend but sometimes she acted funny. She said did we have family problems. I said a few. I caught the bus all right and got home early Saturday night. Mom was sick in bed and Dad gave me a dirty look when I got in but it was a quiet night and I got a little work done, also watching *Monty Stratton Story* on The Late Late Show after Dad went to bed.

I went to an A.A. meeting with Mom. Alice picked us up and drove us over. They had the meeting, with the A.A. prayer, then refreshments of coffee and cake. Alice was in charge of refreshments. A lot of people said hello to Mom, calling her Clare, and it seemed like she never had so many friends before. Three people (one woman and two men) told the story of what drinking did to their lives and how they finally stopped. The first man was divorced because of his drinking and not allowed to see his children as he had beat up his son. All three had the DT's a few times. The woman described the kinds of animals she saw, saying if they were only pink elephants it wouldn't be so bad. Practically everyone laughed as they had had the DT's. (Mom hadn't had them then.) A member had to be sober three months before he could speak. Mom said even if she got that far she wouldn't like to talk in front of everyone. I had a cup of coffee with Mom for old times sake. Everyone at the meeting was nice (except Jean). I was avoiding her and she was avoiding me. Everyone said I looked just like Mom.

Mr. Drescher gave us our choice of biographies and I chose Robert E. Lee to please Mom. I read one book all the way through and skimmed a couple of others. Lee was the old-fashioned general who lived by the gentlemen's code. The North wanted him to lead the Union troops but he loved his home state, Virginia, and couldn't be disloyal. The North took Grant who graduated about last in his class at West Point. Lee had to rely on surprise tactics as the South was outnumbered and had almost no factories. When they were blockaded it slowly choked them and soon the Confederate army was in rags and half starving. Lee thought his only chance was a quick victory but when the charge at Gettysburg failed, the South began to retreat. Grant didn't have to think about great tactics—he had the men and equipment so he just kept wearing him down. He didn't live by "the gentlemen's code"—he drank and swore, he just thought of it as his job to win the war. The South kept fighting even after it was a lost cause, and finally Lee surrendered when he saw it would only mean more of his men killed if he kept on. At the surrender he offered Grant his sword. Grant wouldn't accept it—which showed he could be the gentleman too. Mom told me Lee didn't burn the crops in Pennsylvania, but the North burned everything when they came into Georgia and Alabama. (I put that in the report.) They set the cotton warehouses on fire and people could see the flames in the sky for miles. Nonny (my Aunt Sally's mother) saw them when she was small.

When I was in my second year of high school, Celia died. I didn't expect anything. The dean called Dad Sunday night. We didn't know what to do, we couldn't even believe it was true. I was just doing my homework, Dad was watching TV, and Mom was sleeping when the phone rang. It was like a bad dream to me. Dad answered the phone and started saying, "What? What?" He told me to wake up Mom, telling me something had happened to Celia. He was asking the dean where she was and how it happened, and was he sure it was her. I thought it was a car accident. I woke up Mom telling her something had happened to Celia at school. She got up right away; she was wide awake as she could tell it was serious with me crying and Dad on the phone long distance. I had a terrible feeling something bad had happened. I was afraid to listen to what was going on. I ran in my room and lay on the bed holding my ears. Finally Mom came in and told me what it was, although I kept

149

yelling to drown her out and put the pillow over my head. I gave her a bruise on the shoulder kicking her.

We stayed at a motel by the college, getting up there around ten. We were going to leave Johnnie with Mrs. Bundy but we left too early. I stayed with him at the motel. Dad had to call work from a pay phone on the way up as he had an important meeting. They had to talk to the dean and the doctor plus some other people and get the report of what happened. There was a coffeeshop attached to the motel and I went over with Johnnie for lunch. We both had hamburgers with milk for him and tea for me. Mom told him Celia went away on a long trip but he didn't know what it meant. He probably thought she was coming to lunch since everyone was talking about her. Mom drove back with sandwiches as she didn't know there was a place in the motel. Dad was still at the college. She said they already saw a minister and the funeral was going to be the next day. She had a cup of coffee, acting completely sober as though she knew what to do. I wished she could be like that all the time. She was nice to me, not even saying anything about the marks she had, which showed when she was trying on a dress. She had to buy a black dress for the funeral as she didn't have one. I went with her, taking Johnnie too. The stores there were small. The first two didn't have anything black but the third one did and it fit Mom all right. The lady said they would alter it but Mom wanted to take it with her and do it herself. The lady said they would have it ready in the morning, but Mom said it would be impossible, as she needed it early as her daughter died yesterday and the funeral was in the morning. She started crying but stopped right away. The lady said she would alter it immediately
150

and her husband would bring it to the motel before six.

Mom went to pick up Dad at the college. We all had supper at the motel, and after that the minister came to talk to Mom and Dad. He was younger than Rev. Lanford and half cheerful, half sad. He said the comfort of the afterlife doesn't mean as much when the person is so young. He told them what would happen at the funeral. It was a pretty short ceremony. Mom and Dad thanked him for taking care of the arrangements and keeping the funeral directors away, which they were dreading. He asked what Celia was like and what she was interested in, also whether she seemed like an unhappy person. He didn't know her as she didn't go to church up there. Mom said she had no idea she was so unhappy. The minister said another girl from the college died three years ago the same way. It turned out she was worried about exams and behind in all her work and took sleeping pills in despair. Dad said Celia was up in everything, as the dean had all her records checked. Mom asked the minister if he thought it was really suicide, since she had tried to call someone. He said he didn't know but it wasn't an important question in our religion. Mom said she was glad she would be buried in Massachusetts as she liked it there. There was no point in bringing her back to New Jersey as we might move away any time, and our relatives were scattered all over the country, far from us or the college. After the funeral we went to the dormitory to get her things. None of her friends were around, probably embarrassed to see us. Jeanne's room was open but no one was there. She and Anna were at the funeral with some others but I wasn't standing near them. We took everything from the bookshelves, the chest of drawers, the

151

desk, and the closet. It only took about a half hour. Most of it fit into her two suitcases and the rest we got into the back of the car with me.

After we got home everything got back to normal again although Mom and Dad stopped drinking for a few days. We were used to Celia not being home so in a way nothing was different. I stayed home two weeks, not doing much but watch TV, read magazines, and sleep. Mom and Dad didn't tell me to go back to school. I didn't really do anything but I slept a lot. The house was a mess but I didn't do any housework.

On Saturday Dad had the idea of going up to Bear Mountain Park. Mom made sandwiches which we had along the way. I sat in the back with Johnnie. The roads were fine as there was no snow yet and there wasn't much traffic once we got on route 9. Hardly anyone was up there. They had a part of the mountain for ski jumps but naturally no one was there with no snow. We walked around and finally went in the lodge. It was warm there, one section was open with a few people at the tables. Mom had some new slacks on with one of Dad's old white shirts and a sweater over that. It looked quite cute. Mom, Dad, and I had coffee and Johnnie had hot chocolate, plus he and I both had apple pie à la mode. It all came to about $1.50. We went for a walk by the lake. It wasn't frozen over yet. It was icy in parts but not hard enough for the ice skaters. They had winter sports there but it had to get colder. It was freezing when the wind blew, the baby's teeth were chattering by the lake and his nose running too. We got back into the car and just drove around the mountain roads looking at the views of the Hudson River and other mountains. I had a library book with me, *From Here to Eternity*, which I read on the way back until it got too dark.

I had all Celia's clothes in the closet with mine, not knowing what to do with them. I didn't have too many winter clothes so I was wondering if I should use any. There were two plaid skirts with matching sweaters, blue and green, plus some other sweaters, two straight skirts she made by hand, and two blouses, one white and one printed. There were naturally even a lot of slips, pants, bras, knee socks, and pajamas, some new. Mom just wanted to keep a bracelet she always wore. Celia had nice taste in clothes and I was surprised she had so many. It must have been that campus job she had plus money from the summer.

I went back to school before Christmas vacation. Everyone knew what happened probably because Peter Deller told. It wasn't in the papers, I think because all the official reports were in Massachusetts, not New Jersey, and that's how they get the news of deaths. My teachers in every subject told me to see them after school for make-up since I was out two weeks and the marking period was going to close after we got back from vacation, then midterms. Miss Terry (English teacher) said she would give me a long extension as they were practically finished with *Silas Marner* and already working on projects. Miss Bristol (geometry) recommended just the opposite, that I should make up all the work right away and it would be the best thing for me. They all had different ideas about what I should do. The two men teachers gave me cards with a list of what to do. Mr. Gallo gave me hints of what to study for the history midterm, saying to keep it to myself. Celia was taller than me but I could still wear her things as they wore them short at college and it was still the "new look" in high school. I wore her blue outfit when school started after the holidays, January 3, then I gradually started wearing the other things, mixing her sweaters with my skirts, etc. It was a big relief to have so many clothes and not worry about what to wear in the morning. I started wearing everything, even the underwear that fit me. The bras were too big but everything else was okay. I think I was more popular because of the clothes. Two guys, Ronny Zengler and Dom Strassa, started walking with me between classes and they never talked to me before.

I had to see Mr. Graham again for vocational guidance. He wanted to know my interests and how they were changing in high school. I told him I still hadn't settled on anything. He asked me about my preference in colleges—all girls or co-ed. I said probably co-ed, and not too far from home. He said I didn't have to decide right away what I wanted to be, as college gave you time to think about your major, but I should try to narrow down on what school in the next year or two. I asked him what kind of things you could do if you didn't go to college. He said get a job, but not such a good one.

I went over to Bergen Mall shopping center on Saturday. It was only walking distance from my house although most of the people came by car from all around. There were big parking lots spread out around the stores, full of cars. They had a Bambergers, Gimbels, Woolworths, Howard Johnson's, Sam Goody's, National's, Kitty Kelly, A. S. Beck, plus a lot of small stores. On one arcade they even had an optician's office, photographer's studio, and custom bridal dresses shop. I went over with Sue who had to get white heels. She finally found what she wanted at Beck's, then we went to Sam Goody's and looked at albums. After that we split up as she had to get home. I walked around the arcades and out around the new bowling alley. They played organ music, making it sound just like the roller rink. They had pay phones in the front arcade and I called home. Mom answered but I thought she was drinking so I just hung up without saying hello. I had an ice cream and walked around some more. Some of the small stores closed at six but the big ones stayed open every night. I went into Bambergers, looking around the stationery department and went on up to ladies' sportswear where Celia worked on her summer vacation from college. They were getting in all the spring clothes. She was in the ensembles section and it was still the same, coordinated outfits, but naturally different clothes than when she was there. The supervisor of the department was the same, yelling about something at the sales desk. There was also a girl who worked there the year before. I used to see Celia talking to her when I came up now and then to meet her after work. I thought she didn't recognize me at first but then she came over and asked me was my sister working there in the summer. I guess she wasn't in the grapevine of friends from school so she had never heard about it. I didn't want to go into it so I just passed it off and said I didn't know. She said she hated the supervisor, who was running her ragged, and was going to quit as soon as she got her spring clothes with her discount. She had to get back to work and I stayed

155

around a while looking at the skirts and sweaters. Then I looked around some other departments— baby's furniture, dishes, towels and bathmats, and some other things. I could have stayed till it closed but I left around 8:30. I had to walk a mile to get off the parking lot but after that it was just a few blocks to get home. There were little streets with old houses but they were hard to cross at night because of all the traffic from the mall. Once I got home I went up to my room and went right to bed but I couldn't fall asleep.

AVON ◆ NEW LEADER IN PAPERBACKS

CONTEMPORARY READING FOR YOUNG PEOPLE

~~~~~~~~~~~~~~~~~~~~~~~~~~~~~~~~~~~~

- ☐ **Pictures That Storm Inside My Head**
  Richard Peck, ed. 30080 $1.25
- ☐ **Don't Look and It Won't Hurt**
  Richard Peck 30668 $1.25
- ☐ **Dreamland Lake**   Richard Peck 30635 $1.25
- ☐ **Through a Brief Darkness**
  Richard Peck 21147 $ .95
- ☐ **Go Ask Alice** 21964 $1.25
- ☐ **A Hero Ain't Nothin' but a Sandwich**
  Alice Childress 20222 $ .95
- ☐ **It's Not What You Expect**   Norma Klein 32052 $1.25
- ☐ **Mom, the Wolfman and Me**
  Norma Klein 18259 $ .95
- ☐ **Please Don't Go**   Peggy Woodford 20248 $ .95
- ☐ **Blackbriar**   William Sleator 22426 $ .95
- ☐ **Run**   William Sleator 32060 $1.25
- ☐ **Soul Brothers and Sister Lou**
  Kristin Hunter 28175 $1.25
- ☐ **A Teacup Full of Roses**
  Sharon Bell Mathis 20735 $ .95

~~~~~~~~~~~~~~~~~~~~~~~~~~~~~~~~~~~~

Where better paperbacks are sold or directly from the publisher.
Include 25¢ per copy for mailing: allow three weeks for delivery.

Avon Books, Mail Order Dept.
250 West 55th Street, New York, N.Y. 10019

CR 12-76

AVON ◆ NEW LEADER IN PAPERBACKS

CONTEMPORARY READING FOR YOUNG PEOPLE

☐ **The Cay** Theodore Taylor 21048 $1.25

☐ **The Owl's Song** Janet Campbell Hale 28738 $1.25

☐ **The House of Stairs** William Sleator 25510 $ .95

☐ **Listen for the Fig Tree**
  Sharon Bell Mathis 24935 $ .95

☐ **Me and Jim Luke** Robbie Branscum 24588 $ .95

☐ **None of the Above** Rosemary Wells 26526 $1.25

☐ **Representing Superdoll** Richard Peck 25115 $ .95

☐ **Some Things Fierce and Fatal**
  Joan Kahn, ed. 32771 $1.50

☐ **The Sound of Chariots** Mollie Hunter 26658 $1.25

☐ **Guests in the Promised Land**
  Kristin Hunter 27300 $ .95

☐ **Taking Sides** Norma Klein 27599 $ .95

☐ **Sunshine** Norma Klein 19935 $1.50

☐ **Why Me? The Story of Jennie**
  Patricia Dizenzo 28134 $1.25

☐ **Forgotten Beasts of Eld**
  Patricia McKillip 25502 $1.50

Where better paperbacks are sold or directly from the publisher.
Include 25¢ per copy for mailing: allow three weeks for delivery.

Avon Books, Mail Order Dept.
250 West 55th Street, New York, N.Y. 10019

CRY 12-76